forever FOUR

by Elizabeth Cody Kimmel
Grosset & Dunlap
An Imprint of Penguin Group (USA) Inc.

GROSSET & DUNLAP
Published by the Penguin Group
Penguin Group (USA) Inc., 375 Hudson Street,
New York, New York 10014, USA
Penguin Group (Canada), 90 Eglinton Avenue East, Suite 700,
Toronto, Ontario M4P 2Y3, Canada
(a division of Pearson Penguin Canada Inc.)
Penguin Books Ltd., 80 Strand, London WC2R 0RL, England
Penguin Group Ireland, 25 St. Stephen's Green, Dublin 2, Ireland
(a division of Penguin Books Ltd.)
Penguin Group (Australia), 250 Camberwell Road, Camberwell,
Victoria 3124, Australia
(a division of Pearson Australia Group Pty. Ltd.)
Penguin Books India Pvt. Ltd., 11 Community Centre,
Panchsheel Park, New Delhi—110 017, India
Penguin Group (NZ), 67 Apollo Drive, Rosedale,
Auckland 0632, New Zealand
(a division of Pearson New Zealand Ltd.)
Penguin Books (South Africa) (Pty.) Ltd., 24 Sturdee Avenue,
Rosebank, Johannesburg 2196, South Africa

Penguin Books Ltd., Registered Offices:
80 Strand, London WC2R 0RL, England

Text copyright © 2012 by Elizabeth Cody Kimmel. Illustrations copyright
© 2012 by Penguin Group (USA) Inc. All rights reserved. Published by
Grosset & Dunlap, a division of Penguin Young Readers Group,
345 Hudson Street, New York, New York 10014. GROSSET & DUNLAP
is a trademark of Penguin Group (USA) Inc. Printed in the U.S.A.

Library of Congress Control Number: 2011014456

ISBN 978-0-448-45548-8 (pbk)   10 9 8 7 6 5 4 3 2 1
ISBN 978-0-448-45612-6 (hc)   10 9 8 7 6 5 4 3 2 1

For Helena Stewart, creator of doors to other worlds tucked in pages—ECK

· chapter ·

1

Who gets in trouble when it's only the second day of school?

Not me. But the kid sitting across from me outside the principal's office was definitely in trouble. I could tell by the way he was hanging his head and scowling at his sneakers. I tried to act like I didn't notice him because this was a very big day for me. I'd been getting ready for it for half the summer. If everything went well with Principal Finley, I might be about to change my entire life.

I started rereading my notes from the beginning, even though I pretty much had them memorized. It was my Big Idea, my shot at seventh-grade fame, my chance to change the world. Well, maybe not the entire world right away. But at least the gym, and maybe the cafeteria. All thanks to a little competition offered by the Curriculum Education Project.

What's the Big Idea, you might ask? A magazine for middle-school girls. Written by me. From the ins and outs of the schoolhouse to the White House, I was going to cover it all. What to expect on the overnight field trip. What to expect on the state tests. What to expect from college in five years and from global warming in ten years. The magazine was going to be new and different and undeniably Me. I absolutely could not wait to get started. All I had to do was make a killer presentation, better than anyone else who'd entered a project in the competition.

The troublemaker heaved a giant sigh, and I glanced over at him. I kind of knew who he was—Alan Something-or-other. He was a year ahead of me, spazzy, and perpetually over sugared. I wondered what he'd done this time. Last year he snuck a plastic cockroach onto the faculty cookie tray. From what I heard, it caused quite a scene. Teachers still inspected each chocolate-covered treat for signs of life before taking a bite.

Alan caught me looking and gave me a glare, so I shifted my gaze to the bust of George Washington by the door. I gave our Founding Father a little wink. I feel like George Washington would be psyched about my plans to change the world with my magazine. I'll bet he would have been Team Paulina all the way.

The door to the hallway flew open with a bang, and I jumped with a guilty start. Nobody wants to be caught winking at the bust of a departed president. But the girl with wild, blond curls barreling through the doorway didn't seem to notice. She fixed her enormous blue eyes on me and placed one hand over her chest.

"There is a *bat* in the music room!" she exclaimed breathlessly. "A crazed bat! I saw it with my own eyes, and it tried to attack me! I barely got out of there alive!"

Tally Janeway. She was Theater Club Royalty. A bubbly explosion of drama usually surrounded her, like a can of Coke someone's little brother had shaken up. The bigger the drama, the bigger Tally's southern accent grew. Right now, it was as thick as icing.

"A bat?" I asked. Alan folded his arms across his chest and made an "I Am Ignoring You Both" face.

Tally nodded and started pacing the room.

"I know, right?" she said. "In the music room! And it came right at me—all flappety wings and pointy teeth. I'm tellin' you, that bat wanted me *dead*!"

Tally drew out the last word—*dayyyuddd*. She stared at me, her eyes huge, waiting for my reaction.

I wasn't really sure what to say. She *might* actually have been chased by a murderous bat, but knowing Tally, it was also more likely she'd just seen a very large bee.

"That sounds crazy," I said. So crazy, I wasn't sure how else to respond.

Tally stopped pacing and pointed a finger at me.

"Paulina, that is *exactly* what it was. Cuh-razy. Hey, am I late?"

Tally and I were friendly enough, but we weren't actually *friends*. So I had no idea if she was late or not. I didn't even know why she was here.

"Well," I said carefully. "I guess that depends on what you're here for."

"Paulina Barbosa, that is deep," Tally declared. She fixed Alan with a look, like she was expecting him to weigh in on my unexpectedly philosophical observation. He just folded his arms tighter and closed his eyes.

Tally plunked herself down in a chair and immediately looked sleepy. When she was right in the middle of a huge yawn, the door opened again.

Miko Suzuki walked into the room. I gulped. While Tally was regular-people popular, Miko was Big-Time Popular. Tally knew my name and talked to me every once in a while. Miko knew my name and pretended I didn't exist. If I had to make a list of people I was afraid to rub the wrong way, Miko Suzuki would definitely be on it. She and her friends could turn your life into a nightmare if they got mad at you. Ask Suzie Gunderson, who made the World-Class Mistake of laughing out loud when Miko accidentally sat on a cupcake during the fifth-grade

Christmas pageant rehearsal. After that incident, Suzie endured four solid months of finding icing spread on her stuff, including her hairbrush. It was enough to turn a person off from cake for a very long time.

I looked at Miko without seeming like I was looking at her—a little trick I've gotten good at over the years, since it's never a good idea to initiate eye contact with someone like Miko. People have gotten their lockers toilet papered for less.

Miko was picture-perfect, as always. What did she do to get her hair to look so smooth? How did her lip gloss stay on so evenly, without any smudged to one side?

I sighed quietly.

Miko hung out with the other picture-perfect girls I secretly called Prom-Queens-in-Training. PQuits. The pecking order was very clear. I was sort of a Brain. And Brains weren't supposed to say hello to PQuits without the PQuits saying it first. Unless they were looking for trouble. And I did. Not. Like. Trouble. So I didn't say anything at all.

Miko glanced at me, then looked at Tally. Alan was apparently completely invisible.

"Hi, Tally," she said, taking a seat exactly halfway between the two of us.

"Hey, Miko," Tally responded brightly. "Did you hear about the bat in the music room?"

"I heard it was a mouse," Miko said.

"It was a *bat*," Tally corrected her. "A huge one. I'm pretty sure it bit me. I could have rabies, y'all. I could turn into a vampire!"

As Tally rambled on about the size of the bat's fangs, how long it took the average girl to become a vampire, and whether vampire bats and vampires were actually the same thing, Miko looked at me again. It seemed like she was trying to decide whether to say hello. Or whether she knew my name. Or if I was a Brain or an Outcast. It was all an act, though. Miko and I had been at the same school since kindergarten. She knew exactly who I was—she was just pretending not to remember. Classic PQuit move.

". . . or garlic around my neck, but it would smell sooo bad, or a stake through the heart, which is so funny, y'all, because when I was little I thought it meant a *steak* through the heart, like meat, right? And I couldn't ever understand how you could get a steak through a . . ."

Tally's words came faster and faster until they all seemed to run together. Miko rolled her eyes.

"Tal, enough already," Miko said. "You're frying my brain, and I have to concentrate when I go in there to talk to Mrs. Finley."

I suddenly wondered what Miko was doing here. While Tally might or might not be in trouble, PQuits never broke school rules. Or at least they never got *caught* breaking them. So why did Miko need to talk to the principal?

Before I could come up with any theories, the door to the principal's office opened. I stood up as Mrs. Finley came into the waiting area. She was wearing her usual, sensible dark suit, and her graying hair was sculpted into an impeccable bun.

"Good morning, everyone," Mrs. Finley said. She didn't look surprised to see that there were four of us waiting for her. "Alan, you will need to wait a little longer," she said firmly. "I have a scheduled appointment right now."

Something fluttered in my stomach. This was it—the moment I'd been waiting for since July. I walked into the office and sat down in the big chair closest to the desk. I did have a scheduled appointment after all. Miko and Tally would have to wait with Alan.

But to my surprise, Miko and Tally followed me inside. *What were they doing?* This wasn't like open mic night—you couldn't just waltz right in, even if you were a PQuit. I looked at Mrs. Finley, trying to send her a telepathic message that Miko and Tally were not part of my presentation.

But Mrs. Finley didn't say anything. She simply sat down at her desk and pulled out some papers. Then she glanced up to smile at all three of us.

"Let's get started," she said. "You're here because of the applications you have completed for the student competition called the Curriculum Education Project. It's very exciting that this program is available to fund a new student group specifically for girls. As you're obviously aware, we've lost a number of organizations and clubs because of budget cuts. The CEP is giving us a chance to get something back."

I knew all of this. It was all in the package we'd gotten over the summer from the CEP. The most important part was the prize—the project that won would get full funding for an entire year. I felt like my magazine was exactly what they were looking for, and I had a good shot at winning.

"We've had a wonderful response from the middle-school students," Mrs. Finley continued. "I received more submissions than I expected. I distributed all of them to the faculty and school board, and we have selected what we feel are the four ideas that have the most potential."

I peeked at Tally and Miko. So they must have submitted CEP ideas, too. I could imagine Tally wanting to do something theater related. But what kind of idea would a PQuit have come up with?

"Four of the proposals I received were very similar," Mrs. Finley continued. "That is why I have asked to meet with you girls as a group. I'm hoping you'll be able to work as one."

I blinked. *Work as a group? Oh no.* That was not one of my strong suits. Since kindergarten, my otherwise pretty excellent report cards always included the comment "Does not work well in groups."

Mrs. Finley placed four file folders on the desk.

"All of your proposals were for some kind of student publication written and published by girls, for girls. Both the faculty and school board loved the idea. I'd like you to work together on it."

I felt my face flush. This couldn't be happening. This was MY Big Idea! How could other people have come up with the same thing? Especially *these* people? I couldn't work with a drama queen and a Prom-Queen-in-Training. Tally was nuts, and Miko wouldn't even acknowledge my existence!

I could just say no, I thought. Tell Mrs. Finley that I changed my mind about the project. But I had put so much work into it. I was so sure I could do something amazing, make a splash, and change the world. I had even told some people about it—possibly even bragged a little. It would be so humiliating to end up quitting before I even got started.

And something told me Mrs. Finley wasn't asking if I was okay with it. She was telling me I would be. Me, Tally, and Miko would be working together on the magazine as a group. Like it or not.

I did not.

"So your group will be one of the four finalists. The CEP guidelines allow each group a trial period of one month."

"Like an audition?" Tally asked.

Mrs. Finley nodded.

"Exactly," she said. "You will write and publish the first issue of a magazine. You must do all the work yourselves and not get any help from your parents or other professionals. You'll have a budget of one hundred dollars for any costs. The final project will be judged by a faculty and student vote."

A million thoughts rushed through my head. How would I do MY magazine MY way with people like Miko and Tally tossed into the mix? The whole thing was ridiculous.

There was a knock on the door.

As I heard Mrs. Finley call "Come in," I remembered she said she had received *four* similar proposals. But there were only three of us here.

I glanced over at Miko, who had turned toward the door. From where I was sitting I couldn't see who was about to come in, but apparently Miko could. She was scowling for all she was worth.

Wow. Who had earned a PQuit scowl this early in the morning? Even I had just been ignored.

My curiosity got the better of me, and I leaned forward to get a good look.

· chapter ·
2

It was The New Girl. I didn't know her name yet, but in the two days school had been in session, she'd already caused a bit of a ripple. People seemed convinced there was some mysterious story behind her sudden appearance at Bixby Middle School. The PQuits had taken an instant dislike to her and made a point of staring her down on the first day of school. No one seemed to know exactly why they hated her. Or why she had moved here. Some people thought maybe she'd been kicked out of her last school. I had also heard rumors about her having famous parents who'd sold their fleet of limos and yachts and given up the good life so their daughter could reinvent herself away from the big cities.

"Welcome, Ivy," Mrs. Finley said. "Come right in."

I watched curiously as Ivy walked into the office. Her hair was a brilliant, almost cranberry shade of red, cut in a chin-length bob with precisely straight bangs across her forehead. She was wearing black peg-legged pants that looked like they came from the 1950s and a fitted turquoise sweater embroidered with tiny green swirls. Her skin was extremely fair, setting off her eyes, which were a startling pale-blue.

Miko was still scowling at Ivy. I wondered why the PQuits had decided so quickly that they hated her. I thought Ivy looked kind of cool.

"Has everyone met our new student, Ivy Scanlon?" Mrs. Finley asked. "This is Paulina Barbosa, Miko Suzuki, and Tally Janeway. They are all in the seventh grade with you. We've already gotten started, so please have a seat."

"Hi," I said.

Neither Miko nor Tally said anything. Ivy didn't say hi back, but maybe she was just nervous. I sure would have been. The only chair left was a tiny one, the kind made for a little kid. It had arms and a writing surface on one side. Ivy was very tall, and she looked bizarre squeezing into the little thing. Her knees were almost level with her chin, and her body angled forward so that her face was mostly hidden by a veil of hair. Miko made a soft noise that sounded like a snicker. If I were Ivy, I would have felt totally mortified. But she looked like she really didn't care.

"I'll just quickly recap what we've talked about so

far, Ivy," Mrs. Finley said.

My brain went into overdrive as the principal summarized things for Ivy.

There must be a way to get out of this. I can't put together a magazine with three other people, I thought. It was crazy enough imagining working with Miko and Tally, but The New Girl, too? For all I knew, Ivy could be some kind of lunchroom sociopath, like the one in that movie who secretly stalked people and had a collection of big, shiny knives.

"To publish the magazine together, as a group . . . ," Mrs. Finley was saying.

I've got to get out of this somehow, I thought. Wasn't there some hideous, highly contagious bug I could get? Or what if I insisted on some condition nobody else could agree to, like having the magazine be . . . written in French? Mandarin? Or what if I went home immediately and worked all day and night on the magazine myself? I could finish up by morning and bring the entire thing into Mrs. Finley's office, and then I'd just be done with all of it.

"So the four of you will need to sit down and agree on some of the basics: the style and content and the topics you're going to cover in the magazine. And, of course, the name."

The name! Could I maybe insist on a name so terrible that *everyone else* quit the group? Something like . . . *Thinkers' Thoughts? World Economics and Medieval Knitting Monthly? Contagious Skin Conditions and You?*

"So I've arranged for the four of you to meet during lunch today in the small conference room off the library. I must say, I'm extremely curious to see what you four girls will come up with!"

I'll bet you are, I thought grimly. All my brilliant planning, down the drain.

Mrs. Finley stood up as she finished speaking. I stood up, too, and so did Miko and Tally.

Only Ivy stayed seated.

Maybe she's wedged in that tiny chair forever, I thought. *Maybe they'll have to send the fire department to cut her free.* Wouldn't *that* be a great way to start a new school year?

I felt bad that Ivy might possibly be stuck. A really nice person would offer to help. But I just wanted to get out of that office as fast as possible. I was, as my mother liked to say, "out of my comfort zone."

"Thank you, Mrs. Finley," I said.

It was a total lie, obviously. It wasn't a real thank-you because nothing had happened in that office that I was even remotely grateful for. But seventh grade wasn't a place for saying how you really felt. Imagine how much chaos there would be if everybody in middle school started being honest all the time?

Hi, Paulina, how are you?

Actually I am gripped with despair today, and I have a terrible itchy place on my second smallest toe, and I'm a little worried that the milk I had for breakfast was sour, and I'm going to throw it all up about seven minutes into social studies. And how are you?

"Ivy, can you stay behind a moment?" Mrs. Finley asked.

Miko was already out the door, with Tally close behind her. I shot a curious glance at Ivy before following them out of the office.

The way I saw it, there were three reasons Mrs. Finley might have asked Ivy to stay behind. One: She had used her keen powers of Principalian Observation and realized Ivy was trapped in the chair. Two: The trouble rumor was true, and Ivy was going to get an "I've got my eye on you" lecture. Three: As a new student, Ivy was going to get a special, one-time-only Get Out of the Group Free card. I wondered if I could get one of those, too.

I was so wrapped up in wondering why Ivy was still in the principal's office, I didn't immediately notice that Miko was still standing in the waiting room. She was saying something in a low voice to Tally. She stopped talking when she saw me.

"We don't like the new girl," Miko said suddenly.

I realized with surprise that she was talking to me.

"You mean Ivy?" I asked.

It was a stupid question, since obviously Ivy was the *only* new girl, but I was caught off guard.

"Rumor has it she got kicked out of her last school for stealing," Miko said. "We shouldn't have to work with someone like that."

I stared at Miko. I still wasn't sure who the "we" was in the sentence—her and Tally? Her and Tally and *me*?

While I stood there wondering, Tally took a deep breath that signified a Major Speech was about to be delivered.

"Well, to be totally straight with y'all, I once stole Sarah Mackie's Pop-Tarts at snack time and pretended they were mine. See, my mother gave me the same darn corn muffin for snack every day, and I tell ya, each time I saw Sarah unwrappin' one of her Pop-Tarts I'd get about fit to die of hunger, right? And one day she brought in this new flavor, because before then, they'd always been some kind of fruit-inside ones, right? Only on this day, the Pop-Tarts were chocolate. Chocolate filling, chocolate tart, chocolate icing. Just seeing the picture on the wrapper made my teeth hurt. And I know it was wrong, y'all, but I just had a gnawin' and a cravin' for those Pop-Tarts, so I—"

"I'm thinking about bringing this up with Mrs. Finley," Miko interrupted.

I hesitated.

Well, hey, as long as Miko was going to be talking to Mrs. Finley about who should or shouldn't be in the group, maybe there was some way for me to get out of it, too. If Miko hated people who stole so much that she didn't want to work on a magazine with them, maybe I could find something to swipe right here in the waiting room. What if I tucked the bust of George Washington under my arm and liberated him from the school? Then maybe Miko wouldn't want to work with me, either.

But Miko was giving me a very clear "I'm done talking—you're dismissed" look.

If my best friend, Evelyn, had still been at school with me, I might have felt a little more brave. But Evelyn had moved over the summer, and I was going to have to get through seventh grade without her. This did not seem like a good time to be doing anything that might potentially irritate a PQuit. Or anyone for that matter.

Tally looked like she was getting ready to resume her Pop-Tarts confessional.

So I said a quick good-bye and hightailed it out of there.

· chapter ·

3

I obsessed over my new problem through my first three classes. By fourth period I was more worried than ever. My stomach always rumbled a little during social studies because it was right before lunch. Today, though, it was much worse. It was *deafening*. Tally had fourth-period social studies, too, and she was still going on about Pop-Tarts, which didn't help my brain tell my stomach to be quiet.

Halfway through class, Tally had decided to go on a tear about something else, and the teacher, Ms. Zangeist, was waiting for her to take a breath. Or keel over or something.

"So they had to eat bugs or candles or their own shoes or something, and that was just the boat ride over, and then when they got to the fort, they still didn't have enough food, but nobody back home could send over help because they were fighting the

Spanish Ramada, so they ate more bugs—"

"Spanish *Armada*," Ms. Zangeist corrected quietly.

There was some laughter just in time to cover a particularly loud burble from my tummy, so I crossed my fingers and hoped Tally had plenty left to say on the subject of early American colonization.

"And all this time they're waiting for help, but *nobody comes* . . . right? Until finally three years later, a boat shows up to help them."

"Ship," our teacher said patiently.

"Only, y'all . . ." Tally finally looked around at each of us, taking a lengthy pause that had me in an agony of embarrassed anticipation.

"The colonists were *gone*," Tally declared. "Every single man, woman, and child. And there was nothing left but a carving in a tree, which said 'Cryptonite.'"

"It said *Croatoan*," Ms. Zangeist corrected. She was starting to look more amused than impatient. My stomach made a loud, brief noise at a moment when no one was talking.

"Where'd they go?" I asked as loudly as I could.

Tally spun around to face me.

"That's the thing. To this very day nobody knows. They were just *gone*. Like on that episode of *Alternate Universes* when the whole skyscraper gets sucked into the parallel universe and disappears, and the people in the way all get extra arms and legs. One of them even gets an extra head growing out of his chest, and it opens its mouth, but all it says is 'gahhhhh.'"

All rightee then.

"Did the colonists get extra arms and legs?" asked Benny Novak. Then he shot me a look and winked.

What was that? I wondered. And why is he still looking at me? I glanced down and pressed my hands over my belly. Do not growl, I mentally commanded it.

"Nobody knows because they never even found their skeletons," Tally stated. "But here's the thing, y'all. I think I know what happened to the lost colonists of Rowing Oak."

"*Roanoke*," said Ms. Zangeist. "Well, don't keep us in suspense, Tally. What happened to them?"

"Okay, so they were starving, right?" Tally asked. "Like, to death. None of them had eaten a decent meal in years."

A big noise came out of my stomach. It sounded like the possessed girl in that exorcism movie. Why did Benny Novak's desk have to be so close to mine? And why had he winked at me? Maybe he just had something in his eye.

"So here's what I figured out happened: They ate each other," Tally stated confidently. "I'm sure of it. One day they just gave in and started cannon-bulling each other."

"*Cannabilizing*," Ms. Zangeist chimed in.

"Okay, but wait," Benny said. "If they ate each other, wouldn't there have been one person left over? I mean, who took the last bite?"

Is it a bad thing that all this talk about cannibals was making me even *hungrier*?

To my great relief, suddenly everyone was chiming in with a theory about how a bunch of people could simultaneously eat each other and not leave a single person standing. Ms. Zangeist looked like she was trying to regain control of the conversation when the bell for lunch rang. Finally!

I grabbed my books, jumped up, and was out the door before anyone could say anything to me. And by anyone, I mean Benny Novak.

I'd been so obsessed with hiding my stomach growls that I had temporarily forgotten to worry about the CEP meeting scheduled during lunch. I grabbed my lunch from my locker and hurried toward the library, trying not to mutter to myself. I do that sometimes when I'm worried. When I reached the conference room, I saw that Ivy was already there sitting at the table.

At least she got herself a regular-sized chair this time, I thought.

"Hi," I said.

Ivy looked up at me. "Hi," she responded.

I took the chair opposite Ivy, then placed my book bag on the table and rummaged through it to avoid what seemed like an uncomfortable silence. I made a kind of production about first finding a pen and then a notebook in my bag. After I'd placed them both on the table, I'd totally run out of stuff to do.

"I'm Paulina," I said.

"I remember," Ivy replied.

"And you are Ivy," I stated.

She gave me an amused smile, and I noticed for the first time how pretty she really was.

"Yes. I am Ivy."

There was another silence.

"So, you're new," I said.

I realized as soon as the words came out of my mouth I had probably set a county record for stupid remarks. Ivy stared at me with her pale-blue eyes.

"Yep, I am the new girl in town," she confirmed.

She didn't say anything else. She just sat there, cool as a cucumber, watching me. I started flipping through my notebook, where I'd been taking notes in social studies. I reviewed what I'd taken down.

"Colonists at Roanoke, where did she even get that, but it might be on the test . . . people eating each other, come on . . . like, way to start a country, guys, treating each other like appetizers . . ."

Oh no. I was muttering again.

And Ivy was watching me.

"Got a little sidetracked in social studies today,"

I explained, pointing at my notes like that would clear things up. "A little unexpected cannibal talk. Probably didn't need to put that in my notes. I mean, if you write down everything people say, you go nuts. Not you, I mean. I do."

"Sure," Ivy said.

Like, you *sure* sound nuts to me.

I will now keep my mouth closed, I commanded silently. I will say nothing. Eventually someone else will show up.

I hope.

· chapter ·

4

At that moment Tally blew through the door like she'd been shot out of a cannon.

"Am I late?" she said breathlessly. "Any news on the bat? Has it killed anyone? Did I tell you it went straight for my neck? Do either of y'all see any puncture wounds on my skin?"

I had never been so happy to see Tally Janeway in my life.

"No visible punctures," I said. "I think you're going to be okay."

"What a relief!" Tally declared, pulling out a chair next to me and plopping down. Ivy watched her, an amused expression on her face.

"There was a bat in the music room," Tally explained to Ivy.

"I heard something about that," Ivy replied.

"A vampire bat, probably," Tally added.

"Vampires suck," Ivy said.

I laughed.

"That's funny," I said.

"Thanks," Ivy replied. She smiled at me.

"I don't get it," Tally began. "What's—"

She stopped talking as Miko walked into the room.

"So I don't have a lot of time," Miko said immediately. She took a seat next to Tally. "Can we talk about whatever we're supposed to go over?"

Hmmm. I wondered if Miko had talked to Mrs. Finley or not. Either way, it looked like she was going to have to work with Ivy. Which meant *I* was going to have to work with all of them.

"Oh, y'all, we have to *win* this, right?" Tally exclaimed. "We'd be famous! At least in school. Hey, maybe they'd come do one of those reality shows about us. Wouldn't that be amazing?"

"The first thing we need to do is find out who the other three groups are," Miko said. "We need to know what we're up against."

"I heard one of them is a sports team," Tally said.

"I heard that, too," Ivy added.

Miko gave Ivy a surprised look as if she wondered who Ivy would have heard anything from.

"So we need to figure out what the other two groups are doing," Miko said. "We should know that before we make any decisions about our magazine."

"Why?" I blurted out. Then I remembered my extremely important policy of never speaking to a PQuit unless spoken to first. I braced myself for the PQuit glare.

"Because until we know who our competition is, we won't know how to shape the magazine," Miko said.

Phew! I breathed a sigh of relief. Miko was all business today. I might get through this meeting after all. How I'd get through the next four weeks, though, was the big question.

"If we stay true to the original vision to create a magazine as the voice of all girls, our competition doesn't make any difference," Ivy said.

Uh-oh. Ivy didn't know about the PQuit pecking order. Maybe I should have explained that while we were waiting for the other girls to arrive.

"That's your opinion," Miko said, tucking a long, silky strand of hair behind one ear.

"Well, yeah," Ivy agreed.

A brief silence fell over the table. *This is not going very well,* I thought.

"Well, one thing we definitely need to do is come up with a name for the magazine," I said.

"Oh, I have one," Tally said eagerly. "Let's call it *Applause.*"

"No way," Miko said.

I was glad to hear Miko say it. I did not like that name at all.

"I think we should go for something like *Pink*," Miko continued. "Girl magazine, girl color."

"I hate *Pink*," Ivy said.

I wasn't sure if Ivy meant she hated the name or the color. But it was fine with me either way. I hated them both.

I had actually put a lot of thought into a name. I took a deep breath and tried not to look nervous as I said, "What about something more academic, like . . . say . . . *Scholastica*?"

"Oh, that's awful," Tally said as soon as the words were out of my mouth.

"Terrible," Miko added.

"It sounds like a lost continent for students," Ivy chimed in.

Tally giggled.

Well then. I tried not to blush. Have you ever tried not to blush? It's like trying not to have a face stuck on the front of your head.

"We don't want anything academic sounding," Miko stated matter-of-factly.

We didn't? I did. That was part of my Big Idea, so people would know my magazine was supposed to be taken seriously. This wasn't some rag to read one day and stuff in a pair of wet shoes the next. My magazine was supposed to change the world.

"My proposal was actually for a fairly academic publication," I offered, a little timidly. "Current events, political issues, health topics . . ."

I could tell my face was still red. And turning redder by the second as the other girls looked at me.

"Mine was for a fashion-forward, spot-the-trends kind of thing," Miko said.

"Well, my proposal was for something like a celebrity magazine, except we're the celebrities," Tally chimed in. "Like, who all's going out with who, and what the buzz is each week. With an advice column and theater reviews, too."

"My vision was more like a *Vanity Fair*," Ivy said. "Which has some of everything you guys have said. But with flair."

What is flair? I wondered. *Where do you get it, and how do you know when you have it?*

"I know that magazine. Wasn't the cast of *Glee* just on their cover? Or was that *Life & Style*? I just love Lea Michele," Tally said. "If I could sing like that, I'd die."

"Maybe we should just start with assigning job titles and responsibilities, you know what I mean?" Ivy interrupted. "We'll need a designer, a publicity and marketing director, an editor, and a publisher."

Miko stared at Ivy. "According to who?" she asked.

"That's just the way it works," Ivy said with a shrug.

"Which you are an expert on because . . . why?" Miko asked.

I recognized the challenge in Miko's tone. If I were Ivy, I'd start backing up fast.

But obviously I was about as far from being Ivy as it was possible to get.

"Well, for one thing, my mother was editor in chief of *City Nation* magazine," Ivy replied.

I stared at Ivy. *City Nation* was an incredibly cool magazine—it was like part *Rolling Stone,* part *Newsweek,* and part *Vogue.*

"Are you serious?" Tally said. She looked like she was about to faint. "I save every issue of *City Nation* I've ever gotten. They've done interviews with, like, every one of my favorite actors. Has your mom met all those people? Have you? Oh, Ivy, have you met Brad and Angelina and all twelve kids?"

Ivy shook her head, but Tally continued staring at her, her mouth hanging open in awe.

"Whatever. I'll be the designer," Miko announced. "I'm good at stuff like that."

I had sort of thought we'd vote on jobs, but I wasn't going to suggest that to Miko if she was set on being the designer. So far, Miko was being pretty nice to me, and I wanted to keep it that way.

"My mother knows a website where we can

download a free program for design work like this. I'll send you the address," Ivy said.

"Whatever," Miko said, looking at a spot on the wall about three feet above Ivy's head.

"What does a publicity and marketing director do?" Tally asked.

"Spread the word, get us attention, for starters," Ivy said.

"Oh, I'll do that, then," Tally said. "Marketing sounds like shopping, so I'm a natural for that, and I bet I can do publicity. I'm great at spreading the word."

"I'm pretty good with writing and grammar," I said. "I guess . . . I could be the editor."

"You'd be good for that," Miko said.

Whoa. I felt a big, stupid smile cross my face. Had Miko . . . complimented me? I tried to look less exhilarated than I felt, but I could feel my cheeks growing warm again. I was going to be an editor!

"I'll be the publisher then," Ivy said.

"It sounds like you're making yourself everyone else's boss," Miko said, her tone still cool and her eyes slightly narrowed.

I looked back and forth between Miko and Ivy. "Danger! Danger!" sang a little voice in my head.

"Maybe in the real world the publisher would be the boss," Ivy said thoughtfully. "But for our purposes it just means overseeing every task, creating and keeping a schedule, making up any of the writing that doesn't get done, and getting the magazine printed and bound with the budget they gave us."

"That sounds like a whole lot of busy work," Tally said. "And I'm busy enough already. Did you know they're showing an *Actors Studio* marathon on TV tonight?"

"So it seems like we all have our jobs then," I said, ignoring Tally. We didn't have much time left before lunch would be over.

Miko shrugged, and her expression said she'd lost interest in all of us. "Whatever," she said. She pulled out her phone and started texting someone.

Just then, the bell rang.

"Maybe we should take each other's e-mail addresses," Ivy said. "If you three give me yours, I'll send the group an e-mail, and then we can keep working outside of school."

Ivy ripped a piece of paper from her notebook and put it on the table.

Tally leaned over and scrawled her address hastily. "Sorry, I've got bio across campus, and I want to run by the music room to see if they caught the bat. Talk later, y'all!" she said. She grabbed her bag and dashed out the door.

Miko picked up a pen and wrote her e-mail address on the paper, her sleek, straight hair dropping in front of her face like a glossy curtain. When she finished, she dropped the pen like it was something disgusting, then pulled the strap of her bag over her shoulder. She glanced right through Ivy, then looked at me for a moment.

"See you later, Paulina," Miko said before she left the room.

I was amazed that Miko had not only said good-bye to me, but she'd used my name and everything. I was also aware that she'd been making it obvious that she didn't like Ivy one bit. I scribbled my e-mail address on the paper.

I liked having Miko be nice to me. But I was also starting to like Ivy.

"So I'm kind of psyched about the magazine," I said as Ivy put the e-mail addresses from the paper into her phone. She looked up at me when she was done. Her eyes were her most striking feature—I'd never seen a shade of blue that pale.

"I am, too," she said.

"It's really lucky for us that your mom has all this big-time experience," I said. "Not that we can get her help or anything—I know that's against the rules. But it seems like you probably know a lot about magazines."

Ugh. Good job, I thought. *Way to sound like a gigantic kiss-up.*

"I guess," Ivy said. "And it's just as well we can't officially get her input. She's a bit of a control freak. And things can get kind of complicated when your parents get involved, you know?"

I nodded. "I totally know," I said. "My mother is a psychiatrist, so seriously, just answering a question like 'How are you feeling today' can go epically wrong. I've finally learned if I have a weird dream I should never, ever mention it."

Ivy laughed. "Oh, man. I bet you do have some stories. You'll have to tell me sometime," she said.

"Definitely," I replied.

I almost asked if she wanted to come over. But I didn't want to push too fast. I already felt like I had a sign over my head that said JUST LOST BEST FRIEND. VACANCY AVAILABLE FOR IMMEDIATE OCCUPANCY. INQUIRE WITHIN. Better to wait and see how everything unfolded.

"Hey, do you know where the Humanities Center is?" Ivy asked, shoving her things into her bag and getting up.

"Sure, it's on the way to my next class. I can walk you there," I said, trying not to sound too eager.

"Great. I figured you were the one to ask. Tally might have led me to the football field by mistake, and Miko would probably have lured me into the parking lot and glared me to death."

I laughed as I followed Ivy out the door. Whatever

people were saying about her, I thought Ivy was cool. She was funny and obviously smart.

She also realized that Miko Suzuki didn't like her. Not one bit.

And amazingly, she didn't seem to care.

· chapter ·

5

That night, I had my laptop open on the kitchen counter next to my social studies textbook, the accompanying study sheet, and a large bag of raw broccoli. I was simultaneously opening the bag and scanning the chapter on the economic factors motivating the first American colonists. Somewhere in there I was sure there was a sentence that had the words I needed to answer question two. I had reread the same paragraph about four times when I dropped the broccoli on the floor. It rolled in four different directions, leaving trails of green-budded crumbs.

"Rats!" I exclaimed.

I crawled around picking up the broccoli and tossed it all into a bowl. My computer beeped, indicating an e-mail had come in. I put the bowl of broccoli in the sink and let the water run while I opened the e-mail.

We need to figure out a title ASAP. People are starting to ask. What about *Chick Lit*?

I groaned inwardly. I hated *Chick Lit*. But Fashion Maven was obviously Miko. I didn't want to be the one to shoot her suggestion down and risk turning her friendliness to hostility.

I turned off the water, put the broccoli in the steamer, and turned the stove on. Then I went back to my textbook and tried to remember where I'd left off. Had I really only completed one of the questions? Were we going to get this much homework every night?

My laptop beeped again.

Can't possibly live with *Chick Lit*. What about *Luna Girls*? Luna is the Roman goddess of the moon. Powerful, but also in a constant state of change, kind of like us.

I liked the idea of a Roman goddess, but I wondered if people would think *Luna Girls* was too crazy. I didn't want anyone to think we danced around naked under the full moon.

The oven timer went off, indicating it was done preheating. I grabbed the casserole my mother had left out and popped it in the oven, resetting the timer for twenty minutes. Then I turned back to the study sheet. What were those two words I needed? Maybe I should just skip the second question and start on question three.

Beep. Computer again.

▼ **To:** IvyNYC, Fashion Maven, Paulina M. Barbosa
▼ **From:** StarQuality
Subject: Re: Title

Luna Girls makes me think of Luna Bars, which are supposed to be healthy, but they come in flavors like Cookies 'n Cream Delight, which doesn't taste like cookies or cream but is still really good and much better than the fruit-flavored ones that have all that granola stuck in them.

How about *Scooped* for the title?

I didn't like Tally's suggestion, either. I stood frowning at my laptop, then looked back at my social studies textbook. My eye suddenly fell on the words I was looking for—apprenticeship and servitude. I grabbed the study sheet to write the answer down before it left my brain.

The kitchen door flew open and a ninja-shaped blur shot into the room brandishing a Styrofoam weapon. I jumped and knocked my textbook to the floor, losing my page.

"*Blam! Blam!* Die, Alien Lizard Renegade!"

"Kevin! I keep telling you not to do that!" I yelled. "Now you made me lose my place."

My little brother stared at me with absolutely no remorse.

"Something smells," he said.

I sighed. "It's broccoli," I said.

"I hate broccoli!" Kevin exclaimed. He pointed his Styrofoam ray gun at the steamer and fired off a few imaginary shots.

"Mom left us broccoli and tuna casserole for dinner, and that's what we're having."

Kevin stood in the center of the kitchen, frowning. His dark brown hair fell over his eyes in the front and stood straight up in the back. Sometimes he still looked like the innocent little toddler he once was. I had to remind myself that he was ten now.

"I want a burger and fries," he said.

"Yeah? Well, I want a personal assistant," I told him. "Good luck to both of us. Can you set the table? Mom called and said she probably wouldn't be back before dinner, so we have to do this without her."

Kevin spun his ray gun around the room.

"I'm battling the Reptilian Rebellion," he said. "I don't have time to set tables."

"Make time," I said, picking up my textbook and flipping through the pages. What were those words again?

My computer beeped.

"Incoming transmission!" Kevin shouted, leaping toward my laptop. He reached out and tapped a button. "Who's Fashion Maven? Is this a coded rebel communiqué?"

"Move," I said, irritated. "You're not allowed to read my e-mails, and you know it."

▼ **To:** StarQuality, IvyNYC, Paulina M. Barbosa
▼ **From:** Fashion Maven
Subject: Re: Title

Scooped is too gossipy sounding to me. What about *Paper Dolls*? Lots of potential there for different looks.

Paper Dolls was just as bad as the other names. Not that I had done any better. I hadn't made a single suggestion so far. I started to type.

▼ **To:** Fashion Maven, StarQuality, IvyNYC
▼ **From:** Paulina M. Barbosa
Subject: Re: Title

Dear Ivy, Miko, and Tally,

I agree that none of the suggestions so far are working. Maybe we should shoot for something more literary? Jane Austen's books are really popular again, even though she wrote them in the nineteenth century. What about something like *Austen Girls*?

I hit send, then stared at the computer.

"I'm bored," Kevin said. "And I'm starving. When are we eating?"

"Six," I told him. "Did you finish your homework? You know Mom wants it done before dinner."

"I can't," Kevin said. "I need help on the math. You said you'd do it with me."

I sighed. I *had* told him I'd help. Kevin tended to get himself into a panic over math. But I hadn't even gotten halfway through my own homework yet. And there was dinner to deal with on top of all this magazine stuff distracting me. Had I been nuts to get involved with the CEP?

Another e-mail popped onto the screen.

▼ **To:** Paulina M. Barbosa, Fashion Maven, StarQuality
▼ **From:** IvyNYC
Subject: Re: Title

I don't think *Austen Girls* is a bad idea. I love her books.

"So are you going to help me?" Kevin prodded.

"Just hang on a second," I said impatiently. Two more e-mails had already appeared. The first was

40

brief, from Miko, shooting down *Austen Girls*. I opened the second and cheered. "It's from Evelyn!"

"Are we going to do my math now?" Kevin said.

"Just hang on a minute!" I said.

▼ **To:** Paulina M. Barbosa
▼ **From:** Evie2014
Subject: What's up?

Wish you were here, Paulie. We're finally in the new house, which is totally not new, it's about five hundred years old and freezing cold, and I'm pretty sure my room is haunted. Did you get the picture I sent? How's seventh grade? Have the PQuits found a victim yet?

"Paulie," Kevin began. I ignored him as I typed.

▼ **To:** Evie2014
▼ **From:** Paulina M. Barbosa
Subject: Re: What's up?

Is your room really haunted? I could NOT handle that. I got the picture—the house looks nice from the outside. Seventh grade is insane. Remember the CEP thing I told you about? Mrs. Finley stuck me with three other girls to do the project and one of them is . . . are you sitting down? Miko Suzuki!

"Paulie . . ."

"One second!" I snapped.

My computer beeped again.

To: Paulina M. Barbosa
From: Evie2014
Subject: Re: What's up?

Are you *serious*? Does that mean Miko is going to have to actually talk to you? I thought the universe would instantly collapse if a PQuit ever spoke to either of us. At least it's not Alara the Hun, though! Is she still as mean as she was last year?

And okay, I've been dying to ask . . . have you managed to talk to BN yet? Or even just given him a smile????

Argh, my mom is calling. Will e-mail later. And we have to get the video chat thing working! Love you and miss you like crazy!

I missed Evelyn like crazy, too. I really didn't know how I was going to make it through the year without her. The only thing I could imagine worse than seventh grade itself was seventh grade with No Best Friend.

I was starting to click on the second e-mail when I smelled something burning.

"What the—" I turned and saw smoke coming from under the pot of broccoli. I dashed to the stove and yanked the smoking pot off the burner.

"I tried to tell you," Kevin said innocently.

"Great," I said. "I forgot to put water in the steamer. This is ruined now." I dropped the pot in the sink and ran some cold water over the mess.

"No," Kevin whispered. His tone alarmed me. I look over at him. He was standing by the countertop, his hand over his heart.

"Not the . . . broccoli. *Please* . . . tell me we haven't burned the broccoli!" He gasped. "I cannot live without it!"

He hurled himself to the kitchen floor, went through a series of convulsions, and "died."

"We've burned the broccoli," I told him. "No vegetable with dinner."

Kevin shot up, instantly alive again, a huge grin on his face.

"Awesome," he said.

I laughed for the first time that night.

"So will you help with my math now? I can't do it by myself. Dad always used to help me with it."

I glanced over at my little brother and suddenly felt a surge of affection and protectiveness toward him. My mother had been working longer hours since the divorce two years ago, and Kevin seemed to end up with the short end of the stick, attention-wise.

"Let me finish reading this e-mail, and then we'll figure out your math homework," I said. "We'll have it done before you know it."

I turned my attention back to the computer and typed.

Dear Ivy, Miko, and Tally,

   I apologize I'm not making better suggestions for the title. Can we meet during lunch tomorrow to figure this out and get started on the writing? I have some ideas already. But right now I'm dealing with burned broccoli, a little brother who's shooting up the kitchen with his Alien Lizard Renegade zapper, and this indecipherable social studies study sheet that is going to take the rest of my natural life to complete, unless my brother's Reptilian Rebellion brings doom and death to the world as we know it before tomorrow morning.

I hit Send, then turned to my brother. "Okay," I told Kevin. "Get your math book."

"Affirmative, Commander," Kevin declared. He bounced out of the kitchen like a rabbit on Red Bull, shouting, "Death to Alien Lizard Renegades!"

I checked my computer. One more e-mail.

I'm good for lunch tomorrow. Paulina, your e-mail is hysterical. You're a great writer. I think I'd like to meet this little brother of yours. Maybe we can figure out a time to hang out. Until then, stay low, keep your ray gun fully powered, and don't let the Crusading Crocodiles track you down.

I read the e-mail again. Ivy wanted to hang out. With me.

Kevin came back into the kitchen with his math book under one arm.

"Now?" he asked.

I hit Reply and typed quickly.

▼ To: IvyNYC
▼ From: Paulina M. Barbosa
Subject: Re: Title

Let's definitely hang out. Will see you at lunch tomorrow, unless the Guerilla Geckos smite me in my sleep.

I grinned, closed my laptop, and turned to Kevin. "Okay," I said. "I'm all yours."

· chapter ·

6

Last night's tuna casserole had been pretty bleak eating, but the smell of the cafeteria was even worse. I hate the lunchroom. I mean, I like to eat as much as the next person, but the whole cafeteria experience is kind of nauseating. It's not like I think I'm the center of the universe or anything, but during lunch it sure feels that way. Like everybody is looking at what I'm eating and judging it—too smelly, too messy, too nutritious, whatever. And my mother doesn't help with the ultra-healthy sandwiches she makes. Have you ever tried taking a bite out of a pita sandwich that's stuffed with bean sprouts, cherry tomatoes, and crumbled feta cheese? Let me take the mystery out of it for you—it goes everywhere. Bits of sprouts hang out of your mouth, lumpettes of cheese drop onto the front of your shirt. Dollops of dressing on your chin. Your basic nightmare.

And this year everything was twice as bad about lunch because with Evelyn gone, I had no one to sit with. Having someone to sit with every day is like having a force field around you. The horror still surrounds you, but you can avoid taking direct hits.

I was standing by the milk cooler, holding my brown bag like it was a baby and I was surrounded by ruthless kidnappers. I would have just surrendered to the panic and taken my lunch to the library, but we were supposed to be having a CEP meeting. I hadn't seen any of the other girls yet, but I knew Ivy had to be here somewhere. I stood there like a statue as people walked around me. The air smelled of ketchup and burned pudding, and the many voices chattering sounded like a rainstorm. Every once in a while a few words became distinguishable. "No, he did not!" "Yes, he did!" "No way he did!" "Yes way he did, I swear!" And from another direction: "Crazy, when he was a rookie in the minor leagues!! They'll never make it to the series!" I was starting to feel hopeless when the crowd seemed to part for a moment. I caught sight of Ivy and Tally sitting at a small table near the back of the room.

I headed toward them, passing the PQuit table on the way. Miko wasn't there, I noticed. None of them even glanced up as I walked by. Shelby Simpson was telling a story that had them in stitches.

Ivy looked up and smiled when she saw me. She had on a fitted jacket of deep green with embroidered dragons on it. I had never seen anything like it. Her lunch was laid out on a tray in front of her: a miniature carton of Cap'n Crunch, a banana, and a carton of Yoo-hoo. I could only *dream* of my mother sending me to school with a lunch that good.

"Hi, Paulina," Ivy said. "So you survived the Reptilian Rebellion."

I laughed as I sat down. "Yep. My home remained utterly lizardless all night long."

"What lizards?" Tally asked, looking instantly intrigued.

"We had a slight infestation of armed reptilian rebels," I said, opening my bag and pulling out its contents. "But my brother managed to slay them with his Ray of Doom."

"That sounds terrifying," Tally said with a shudder. "That could get you on the Oprah network."

"I hate Oprah," Ivy said, popping a piece of Cap'n Crunch in her mouth.

"Nobody hates Oprah," Tally said seriously. She looked scandalized that Ivy had even said it.

"I do," Ivy said. "She's a self-righteous, judgmental manipulator who exploits people emotionally while pretending to have the soul of Mother Teresa."

Before Tally could come to Oprah's defense,

something whizzed through the air and bounced off our table.

"Grape," Ivy said. "Close-range artillery. This is Ivy Scanlon, reporting live from the cafeteria front, where sporadic firing continues."

I laughed. Ivy was really cool. I couldn't help but hope that we actually would hang out sometime outside of school and the magazine.

"So I don't know where Miko is, but we should probably get started," Ivy said. "What are we coming up with for content?"

"Okay, I've got a ticket to see the Towne Players's production of *The Secret Garden*," Tally said. "They're our local community theater, and they cast girls my age sometimes. This fourth-grader, Devon Barrow, is playing Mary. What a great part—if I wasn't too old I would have auditioned for it, except the Yorkshire accent is killer, and Devon is from New Jersey, and she says "dawg" and "cawfee," so I don't know how she's going to manage a Yorkshire accent without turning it into a big hot mess, unless she gets a dialect coach, but they're soooo expensive, and sometimes they can make you sound worse than you did before. I mean, dialects can be dangerous, y'all! So I thought I'd go see Devon and write up the show and kind of feature her in the article. Unless she's just awful. I read a review once where this guy wrote that this actress's voice was so irritating the audience all sat with their hands pressed over their ears whenever she came onstage, which I don't think really happened, except it might have because one time I saw a—"

Tally's speech was halted by another grape that whizzed past her head. If she hadn't ducked, I think it would have beaned her. "What was that?" she cried, looking around the cafeteria frantically.

"A piece on Devon and the play sounds great," Ivy piped up. I was grateful that she'd interrupted—Tally could have gone on for the rest of the day. "What are you thinking about doing, Paulie?"

Whoa. Paulie was a nickname only my family and Evelyn used. But hearing Ivy say it, like she'd said it a million times before, made me even more hopeful that we could be *real* friends.

I took a deep, calming breath before telling Ivy about my ideas. I was sort of psyched to be asked because I'd picked some really good ideas from the notes I'd made over the summer. I pulled a little notebook out of my pocket and flipped it open.

"I've got a couple of ideas, but the one I'm really interested in is on this Chinese dissident who won the Nobel Peace Prize, but he's in prison and nobody can talk to him, and it raises this really interesting issue of censorship and human rights on a global level. I'm thinking about things like what our responsibility is to him, and how has he been affected by winning this prize, and could it even be damaging to him personally since he's already considered politically dangerous by his government."

Ivy nodded slowly. "I read about that," she said. "It's a pretty hot topic."

I smiled.

"But the thing is," Ivy continued, "it's not really something that fits with what we're doing. I mean, the whole point is to focus on issues that are immediate for us—for girls our age in this school, right? I'm not sure that a political prisoner in China is what's on girls' minds today."

My smile faded. Of course, Ivy was right. And not just with that idea. The two others I'd sketched out, one on global warming and the other on health insurance, were more Seven O'Clock News than Seventh Grade. That left me with a big, fat nothing.

"Well, I'll tell you what's on my mind today," Tally interjected. "It's that social studies teacher of ours— Ms. Zightgiste. Y'all, she seriously hates me! I know for a fact she's making it her personal mission this year to squeeze the very life out of Tally Janeway. I don't know if anybody has ever died of American history poisoning, but I swear to you, I may be the first to go! Then you could write about me, Paulina. You could tell the sad story of my tragic demise."

I nodded to Tally, but I couldn't stop thinking about what Ivy had said about my story. "No, you're totally right," I said to Ivy. "I'll rework my other ideas and come up with something better."

"Cool," Ivy said. She pointed across the cafeteria. "Oh, there's our missing person."

I turned around.

Miko was standing by the PQuit table, looking perfectly put together as usual. She had on a deep-blue sweater with little, silver buttons and a long, skinny scarf of blues and purples looped around her neck. Her skinny jeans were tucked perfectly into her boots. Did the girl have a team of stylists following her around? I just couldn't see how else a person could look so flawless all the time.

Miko was listening to Shelby, who was still excitedly telling a story. Then she caught sight of us. More specifically, she caught sight of Ivy. Her face darkened in a scowl.

"What is she doing?" Ivy asked. "Lunch is practically over. Does she not see us waiting for her?"

"Miko, come on! We're brainstorming!" Tally yelled.

I put my hand over my face, embarrassed. The entire PQuit table was now looking at us. Shelby Simpson was glaring at Ivy. I felt bad that Ivy had so quickly become the object of the PQuits hatred. What could she possibly have done?

Miko walked over to our table with an irritated look on her face. She pulled up a chair and plopped down in it, placing one pointy booted foot on the empty chair next to her.

"Okay, I'm here," she said. "You don't have to shout at the top of your lungs."

"Oh, that wasn't the top of my lungs," Tally said cheerfully. "When I really shout, you can hear me all the way to Georgia. You have to know how to project when you're on the stage. Once I was on a train going to see my aunt and I—"

"You were projecting just fine," Miko interrupted. "The entire school heard you. What do we even need to talk about? I e-mailed my notes for the design layout."

"We were talking about what articles each of us is going to write," I said.

"Some fiction or poetry would help round out the content," Ivy said.

"I think so, too," I said. "Something creative would go nicely with a theater review and a hard-hitting news story." If I could come up with one that would appeal to the seventh grade.

"Fine, I'll do a short story or a poem," Miko said.

"Okay then," Ivy said. Miko looked at her coolly, her deep-brown eyes slightly narrowing.

Tally sat up straight and smacked her forehead.

"Oh, y'all, I forgot to say I heard about another one of the four groups. They want to do something with a humanitarian group overseas and sponsor a girl our age. You know, like one of those Feed the Children programs where you get a picture of a kid and you can write them letters and send them Hershey bars and stuff? Isn't that kind of amazing?"

"I heard that, too," Ivy said. "They want to start with sponsoring one girl, then try to develop a sister relationship between our school and theirs."

It sounded like an amazing idea. That group had a vision to change the world. I wondered if our magazine would measure up.

"Their idea is great," Ivy said. "But I'm thinking they might not really have enough to go with. My mother and I sponsor two Tibetan kids. We send letters and little treats, and we get letters from them every couple of months. But in reality, there's not all that much to do. To justify a club that's going to win funding, I think you have to come up with more than exchanging letters and pictures. They could accomplish that in one hour a month. What does the club do the rest of the time?"

"Good point," I said, feeling relieved.

"They're never going to be able to pull it off," Miko said, playing with her scarf. "Jenny Nolan and both the Cartwright twins are the ones doing it, and all they do is argue. If those three can even pick a country it will be a miracle."

"If we win, we could find an organization to feature in the magazine," Ivy said. "Maybe the one my mother and I go through, Tibet Aid. Something like that. We could write about them, include a couple of profiles of kids who needs sponsors, let people know how to go about it."

Ivy was full of good ideas. And so far, I'd come up with nothing. *Think!* I thought.

I blurted out the first idea that popped into my head.

"We might also want to think about starting a blog," I said.

Ivy's eyes widened. "That is a fabulous idea," she said. *Good thinking!*

"Yeah. We could use it to create more of a real-time forum where everyone can have input on the magazine or talk about anything. Even put up their own articles or art and post comments. It would help spread the word and give us feedback while we're getting the first issue together."

"I totally agree," Ivy said. "Actually, *City Nation* has an amazing blog. My mother said it increased their readership by ten percent within a month of them launching it."

"Great. Then we can put something up sort of introducing ourselves," I said.

"Exactly," Ivy agreed.

"Well, if you two are done running the world, I'm going to go back and sit with my friends," Miko said.

Ouch. Not that I thought Miko and I would suddenly be besties just because we were working together. Not that I would want to be besties with a PQuit. But still.

"Ta-ta for now," Ivy told her. As usual, she did not seem to notice or care that Miko was unfriendly.

Miko got up without saying anything further and went back to the PQuit table. She sat down and within seconds I could hear them all laughing hysterically. I could hear Miko's voice above the laughter.

"Give me a break—you know I'm only doing it because my parents are making me," she said. "Like I would have picked *those* girls?"

What? I glanced at Tally and Ivy, wondering if they'd heard Miko's comment. Was it true? Was she only doing the project because her parents were making her?

It shouldn't surprise me. But I found myself feeling disappointed.

"Y'all, I'm gonna run, too," Tally said, getting up. "Great jacket by the way, Ivy."

"Thanks. It's vintage. From Korea, I think. I found it at this great little boutique back in the city."

"New York City sounds like heaven." Tally sighed. "I will never forgive myself for not getting there before they closed the Russian Tea Room. They say the new one is totally not the same. Did y'all know Madonna used to work as a coat-check girl there? Can you even imagine that in your wildest dreams? Anyway, see y'all later!"

We watched Tally collide with someone, disentangle herself, and rush to the door.

"She is unique," Ivy said.

"Yes," I agreed. "Often exhausting. Always unique."

The third grape of the hour bounced onto the table in front of me. It rolled toward Ivy's tray and stopped near her Cap'n Crunch. We both looked in the direction it had come from.

Benny Novak was looking at me. I couldn't prove anything in a court of law, but he had a small bunch of grapes on his lunch tray. Circumstantial evidence overwhelmingly identified Benny as the grape thrower. I kept thinking of Evelyn's very basic advice—just smile at the guy! But I never seemed to be able to do it. Even now.

Ivy gave me a curious look. Especially now!

"Friend of yours?" she asked.

I felt my face flush and shook my head. "Friends don't throw grapes at friends," I intoned.

Another grape shot across the table. Ivy smirked. "Sporadic firing continues," she quipped.

I laughed.

The bell rang, and I realized I'd left most of my

sandwich uneaten. Between the work I knew lay ahead for the magazine and Benny Novak's Assault by Grape, my stomach was too jittery for food. I was going to have to budget my time very carefully now. No surfing the Net, no experimenting with video chatting with Evelyn. I had to get myself in high gear.

"Hey, I meant to ask," Ivy said as we headed out of the cafeteria. "Do you want to go to the mall tomorrow and hang out? I understand that's what people do around here on a Friday afternoon. And I could use a guided tour."

"Absolutely!" I said, all plans of getting in high gear flying instantly out the window.

Mall with Ivy: 1. Self-discipline: 0.

· chapter ·

7

On Friday afternoon, I stood outside my mother's office trying to compose myself. I shouldn't have put off asking Mom until today. I'd already told Ivy I could meet her at the mall—what if I couldn't get a ride? I dreaded the hundred questions my mother would ask about Ivy. We might not even end up friends after all. But that wouldn't stop Mom from giving me the third degree.

"Paulina, is that you standing outside my door?" my mother called.

Her sense of hearing was insane. If a kitten yawned in Spain, I bet she could hear it. I walked into her office.

"Hi," I said. "I was just coming to ask you if I could maybe get a ride to the mall today?"

Mom was sitting at her desk in one of her uncomfortable-looking suits. The reading glasses perched on her nose made her look especially severe, but she gave me a bright smile.

"I mean, if you have time," I said. "Otherwise I could ride my bike. I'm just . . . I told the new girl, Ivy, that I'd meet her."

My mother was giving me a look—one of her Psychologist Mom Specials. Like she was thinking very carefully about which of the hundred questions to ask first.

"I'll just take my bike," I said quickly. I started to slowly back out of the office.

"Sweetheart, of *course* I'll drive you," my mother said. She continued to smile at me like I was an experiment she was particularly attached to. Her hair was pulled up in a comb clip, but one gray strand had escaped and was bobbing around like it had something to say.

"Okay, thanks," I told her. "Can we go now?"

My mother nodded, but she didn't move. I knew that look on her face. *Here they come.*

I summoned all the ESP power I had and beamed her a telepathic message—*Do not ask about Ivy! Do not ask about Ivy's parents! Do not ask about Evelyn!*

"So tell me about this Ivy that you're meeting," my mother said.

Note to self: I have no ESP power.

"She's new. She's working on the CEP project with me—one of the three girls I got grouped with. And she

60

asked me to show her around the mall, so I said yes."

My mother nodded thoughtfully. "That's nice. What do her parents do?"

Why do parents *always* want to know what other people's parents do?

"I have no idea, Mom," I said. "Oh, wait—actually she said her mother was the editor in chief at *City Nation* magazine."

My mother's face brightened. "Interesting!" she said. "Do you like Ivy? Are you going to be good friends? You spent so much time with Evelyn, it must be difficult without her. Do you think this Ivy might fill that void a little?"

I don't know what was more irritating, that my mother was asking these questions or that I had already asked myself the same things a number of times.

"I really don't know, Mom," I said. "It's just a trip to the mall."

"Well, come on then," she said as if I was the one holding things up.

My mother talked mostly about planning a spring vacation on the drive to the mall, weighing the relative merits of Florida (sun) versus Washington, DC (culture). I just nodded and offered the occasional "I agree." It was pointless to hope for some sun—culture always won out in the end.

"I guess you don't want me to come in with you,"

my mother said as she pulled up at the front entrance.

I wanted her to come with me slightly less than I wanted an asteroid to be hurtling toward the earth.

"That's okay," I said. "I'll call your cell when I'm ready to go. Around six, okay?"

My mother was scanning the front walk, probably hoping for a glimpse of my new friend.

"Six is fine. Have a good time, sweetheart."

"Thanks, Mom," I said. I hopped out of the car and headed toward the entrance.

The smell of french fries from the food court hit me as soon as I walked through the main doors. Evelyn and I had spent most Friday afternoons here, discussing the school week while sipping on Slurpees and nibbling oversized chocolate chip cookies.

Ivy mentioned liking coffee, so I had suggested we meet at the Koffee King, smack in the center of the food court. I hated the thought of being in the food court alone, so I was relieved to see Ivy already sitting at a table writing in a notebook as I approached.

"Hey," I said.

She looked up and smiled. "Hi," she said. "I got you a cappuccino. Do you like those?"

I nodded, even though I'd never had a cappuccino. I had tried coffee before, but it never tasted anywhere near as good as I thought it should, given the world's apparent obsession with it.

"So I guess you found the place okay," I said, sitting down.

"Yep—this is the only mall for miles around," Ivy replied. "No danger of ending up in the wrong place."

She took a sip of her cappuccino. It left a tiny white mustache on her upper lip. I took a sip of mine, too. It was hot and sweet and foamy. I instantly loved it. Hello, coffee!

"So this must be a total culture shock for you, coming from the city to this," I said.

"New York does have just about everything," Ivy said. "But the only mall I ever went to there was the Manhattan Mall, and it was pretty lame."

"You moved up over the summer?" I asked.

"Last month," Ivy said. "My parents bought a farm up here and decided to reinvent themselves. Live the quiet life. Go back to the land or something."

"Do you hate it?" I asked. I didn't want her to hate it.

"Not at all," Ivy said. "But it's definitely going to take some getting used to. I sort of wish they'd bought a place right in town. The farm is out on Route 22, so it's really isolated. I've never heard quiet like that in my life. For the first week I couldn't sleep because there was no traffic rumbling by."

"It's not that old, stone farmhouse, is it?" I asked. "With the big, red barn?"

"That's the one!" Ivy said, looking surprised. "You know it?"

"My mom likes to drive past it when we take the 'scenic' route home," I said. "But it's a beautiful house. I've always thought so."

"Well, you'll have to come over and see it from the inside," Ivy said. "It's still a work in progress, but it definitely has potential."

"I'd love to," I said.

Ivy smiled. Then suddenly, she nodded at something behind me. "Check your six," she said.

"Check my what?"

"Turn around," Ivy explained. "Or don't. The grape hurler is here."

I froze.

"Benny Novak?" I whispered.

Ivy shrugged. "The grape hurler," she repeated. "The one who is *not* your friend."

I chewed on my lower lip. "What's he doing now?"

Ivy began flipping through her notebook as if she were trying to find something she'd written down.

"He's over by Taco Taco," she said quietly.

I sighed.

"This is so embarrassing," I said. I made a split-second decision to confide in Ivy. "The thing is, I kind of had this epic crush on Benny Novak at the end of last year."

"Well, he's cute," Ivy said. "And he's got a great arm. Those grapes were really on target."

I leaned across the table.

"I just could NOT talk to the guy last year," I whispered. "I'd get too nervous. My friend Evelyn— she moved away over the summer—kept trying to get me to at least smile at him. She said if I couldn't start a conversation, at least I could do that. But I couldn't. So Evelyn finally convinced me to let her drop a hint about the end-of-school dance. You know, casually mention that I wasn't going with anyone. See if he took the bait.

"Only the day before the dance we had a fire drill. Evelyn made her move for the hint drop while we were outside, and she was trying to maneuver him over in my direction, when someone bumped into me, dumping a blueberry smoothie all down my shirt."

"Gotcha," Ivy said, trying to stifle a giggle. It was almost funny, looking back on it. Almost. If you weren't ME.

"So he actually starts walking over in my direction, and I backed away like he was emitting toxic levels of radiation or something. And for the rest of the fire drill, any time I saw him, I just moved away. So it must have looked like I was deliberately refusing to talk to him. Evelyn said she would figure out a way to explain it to him at some point. Then she found out her family was moving, and I kind of forgot all about Benny Novak."

"Until now," Ivy said with a grin.

"Until now," I said with a sigh.

"We should do a piece on that in the magazine," Ivy said. "You know, the social politics of dating. Why girls still feel like they can't just ask a guy out if they feel like it."

"Oh, about the magazine," I said. "I came up with a new idea for an article. I was reading this thing online about a girl who made friends with this guy on Facebook who was really nice to her. Then it turned out he didn't exist, and some girl had just made him up to mess with her. She ended up having a total nervous breakdown. I thought maybe I'd write about cyberbullying."

"That is a great idea," Ivy said. "Have you started writing it?"

"Not yet," I told her. "I wanted to see what you thought of the idea first."

"Go for it," Ivy replied. "We need to schedule another meeting with all four of us. Do you realize we only have just over two weeks left to finish the magazine? With all the work we're going to have to do writing the articles, laying them out, and getting them ready to print. All our articles should probably be done by next Friday if we're going to stay on track."

"I know," I said, taking another long sip of my cappuccino. "I'm starting to worry we're not going to have enough time to get everything done. I've got tests next Friday in social studies and bio, and there's an English paper due, too."

"We can do it," Ivy said. "We've just got to keep on top of Tally and Miko. Tally's about as organized as a hurricane, and it's practically impossible to pry Miko away from her friends. It's obvious she doesn't even like being seen in public with us, or at least with me. She's in charge of the whole layout, and if she decides to blow us off, we'll be in big trouble."

"The PQuits are like that," I said. "Her friends. They don't like one another to spend time with anyone outside their group."

"PQuits?" Ivy asked.

"Prom-Queens-in-Training," I explained.

Ivy laughed. "That is too perfect," she said. "Did you come up with that?"

I gave her a sheepish smile. "I did, actually," I said.

"You are hilarious," Ivy said. "Well, I had a PQuit run-in before school even started."

"You did?" I asked, surprised.

"Yep. The blond one—Shelby? My mother and her mother went to college together, apparently. We ran into them at a restaurant right after we moved up here. Shelby was being really rude to this poor waitress. I was listening to her snapping something about her order, thinking how awful she sounded. Then our mothers recognized each other, and there was this happy reunion. They started making plans to get together, and Shelby said she and I should get together, too, so she could tell me who the cool kids were and who the losers were. I basically told her to buzz off."

"So *that's* why Miko doesn't like you," I said. That explained so much. If Ivy had given Shelby the cold shoulder, of course the PQuits would all despise her. "It's practically a capital offense to turn down an invite from a PQuit."

Ivy shrugged. "Guess I'm on popularity death row then," she said. She finished her cappuccino and crumpled the cup.

She really doesn't care, I thought, amazed.

"So, I noticed there's a big sale at H&M. They had a sweater in the window that would look really cute on you. Want to go check it out?"

"Sure," I said. "Let's do it."

Ivy stood up.

"He's looking this way," she said.

I glanced in the direction of Taco Taco as I stood up. Benny was standing by the cash register, looking every bit the jock in black sweatpants and a varsity jacket. Ivy was right. He was looking in my general direction, but when he saw me looking back at him, he turned away.

"Want me to go ask him if he likes you?" Ivy asked

in a stage whisper.

"Don't. You. Dare!" I said.

"Could be field research for that future article on dating," she pointed out.

"No," I replied firmly.

Maybe Benny Novak had forgotten the way I'd treated him like he had the plague during that stupid fire drill. Maybe he even liked me. Then again, he probably didn't. Which was fine. I had too much to worry about as it was.

"Let's shop," I said firmly.

Ivy nodded. "Lead the way, boss."

· chapter ·

8

"It's perfect. Very you."

I examined myself in the mirror and had to agree. Ivy had convinced me to try on a turquoise sweaterdress and a pair of leggings. It amazed me how a simple change of clothes made me look so . . . different. And kind of cool.

"One other thing—I've been dying to do this," Ivy said. She reached over and pulled out the scrunchie I had keeping my hair in a ponytail.

"Look at those curls," Ivy said. "Why would you want to waste those in a ponytail?"

"It's just easier," I said with a shrug. I had always really liked my hair. Evelyn used to make me submit to her flat iron so she could straighten it, but the end result always left my head looking freakishly large.

"What could be easier than letting your hair down?" Ivy asked. "Now, tell me you're going to get this outfit.

Even if it wasn't on sale, you need this."

"I am," I said. "I haven't gotten new clothes in forever."

"So get them all," Ivy said, gesturing at the little pile of outfits she'd helped me pick out.

Ivy was like a fashion-seeking missile. Everything she had grabbed for me to try on looked great. I especially liked the little plaid skirt and doubled layered T-shirt—I never would have thought to try them on. But the sweaterdress was the best, and it was 50 percent off.

"I'll just stick with this, for now," I told her. "It will almost tap out my allowance, and between all the homework and the stuff we need to get done for the CEP, I'm not going to have time to make any extra money babysitting."

"Well, you're a more responsible citizen than me," Ivy said. "I have no self-control when it comes to buying clothes. Are you going to wear it now?"

I thought about it seriously for a minute. Half the school was probably at the mall by now, and it was tempting to show off my new look. But Benny Novak might still be around. Something about changing outfits seemed a little pathetic to me. Not that Benny would have noticed what I had on before. But still.

"Although . . . ," Ivy said. "You might run into that guy again, in which case it could look weird to be in totally different clothes. I mean, if you care."

I sighed. Ivy had totally read my mind.

"I was just thinking the same thing," I said.

Ivy grinned.

"Then change back," she said. "I'll meet you by the register. I want to check out those belts they have."

By the time I'd changed and found Ivy again, she was on her cell phone.

"But it's not even five thirty," she was saying as I counted out my cash.

"I have it all under control," Ivy said, turning in the other direction. "I'm with one of the girls in the group. We went over her article idea . . . yes, it is all going to be done on time."

I took the change and the shopping bag the cashier handed me. I tried not to seem like I was listening to her conversation as I waited for her to finish.

"Fine," Ivy said. "I'll show you all the notes if that will make you feel better. Yep. Okay."

Ivy snapped her phone shut.

"Sorry," she said. "My mother is having a panic attack about the magazine. Moving to the country was supposed to alleviate her stress levels, but she's making up for it by stressing over *my* deadline. She wants to look over everything I do. I'm going to have to run. I'll call you later. Or do you Skype?"

"Sure, I Skype," I said. Theoretically, anyway. I hadn't

actually tried it yet.

"Text me your Skype address," Ivy said, heading toward the exit.

"Bye!" I called as she walked away.

I took my bag and left the store. Now I had a half hour to kill before my mother came to pick me up. Maybe Shoe Barn would be having a sale, too. I didn't really need shoes, but I was suddenly struck with the notion that a pair of little boots would be the perfect finish to my new outfit.

I was headed in that direction when I noticed a group of kids gathered around a table set up near the jewelry place. A tall girl with thick, brown hair tied up in a high ponytail was handing out flyers. She was wearing a bright red shirt that said PITCH IN on the front. I recognized her as an eighth-grader—a sports nut whose name didn't immediately come to mind. She caught sight of me looking at her and bounded over.

"Did you get a flyer? Here. After you've read it, please sign our petition."

I hated petitions. When someone hands you one, how can you refuse to sign it? It's not like you get a limited number of signatures and you might run out. To say no, you have to be actively and cruelly rejecting something, condemning baby whales to be circus performers or puppies to enforced labor.

I examined the flyer.

Sports for girls have come a long way. So why does our girls' softball team have to use the old mitts and bats the boys' team doesn't want anymore?

Why don't we have real uniforms or regular access to the main field?

Why do we have to carpool to our games instead of getting transportation on the school bus?

Our team may be new, but we deserve the same chance to be winners. We can do that if we get funding, and we need your help.

Will you Pitch In?

The girl stood there watching me read, and I suddenly remembered her name. Sasha.

"You go to my school, right?" she asked. "Weren't you in the spring musical?"

"No," I said. "But I was in the debate club last year. It wasn't quite musical comedy, though. More like a tragic farce."

The joke went straight over Sasha's head.

"So will you sign? We're gathering support for a new girls' club. If we win, we'll be funded for the year."

Oh no. I should have realized—this was the group I'd been hearing about. They were CEP competition.

I was thinking about an excuse I could give to beat a hasty retreat. My little brother was lost? My wallet was missing? I was feeling like I might throw up?

I was about to go for the wallet story when my eyes fell on a girl in a Pitch In shirt moving toward the display table.

Alara Jameson. Aka, Alara the Hun.

I think Alara's epic hatred of me started in fourth-grade science class. Our teacher wrote the symbols for carbon dioxide and water on the blackboard and asked if anyone knew what they stood for. Alara said, "H_2O is hot water, and CO_2 is cold water." I made the mistake of not only laughing out loud in class, but also telling a few people about her answer afterward. I only meant it to be a funny story, but Alara heard me talking about it. She. Went. Ballistic. She's got a temper like you wouldn't believe and a mean streak that's practically visible from outer space. Even though that was three whole years ago, she's gone out of her way to do nasty things to me ever since.

Just last spring, Alara dumped a twenty-four-ounce Slurpee into my book bag, destroying my flash drive containing my six-page book report on *Shiloh*. I did not report her. I was more afraid of getting her in trouble and what else she'd do to me than I was of getting my grade docked for turning in the paper late.

Evelyn had come up with the nickname last year

when we were studying Attilla the Hun. Alara Jameson seemed like a modern-day ringer for the fearsome medieval barbarian who attacked and sacked without reason. Evelyn had even made up a little song to go with the name—"Alara, Alara, Alara the Hun—she'll smite you with her bully's breath and eat you when she's done!"

"So will you sign? I have a pen right here," Sasha pressed.

I wasn't sure what to do. I wanted to get out of there before Alara caught sight of me.

My phone chirped loudly.

"Oops! I have to take this. It's a really important call," I said, handing the petition back to Sasha.

I registered the surprised expression on her face for a split second before hurrying away, my cell phone pressed to my ear.

It chirped again. It wasn't a call, it was a text. Either way, I was saved by the bell. I flipped the phone open.

WR IS THE WaND THINGIE 4 ThE WII?

Kevin, my savior. Unfortunately I could not return the favor because I never played the Wii and had no idea where the thing was. Before I could reply, the phone chirped again.

ALSO—GeT STRAWBERRY POPTARTZ.

Ah. The real reason for the texts. A third message popped up.

> **PLEZe, beST NICEST SISSTEr.**

I smiled. Though Pop-Tarts were not officially outlawed in our house, my mother refused to buy them, causing my little brother to experience pangs of Acute Breakfast Treat Withdrawal Agony. I had enough time to run into Target and get him some. An added plus would be putting additional distance between me and Alara. I headed into the store.

I found the frosted, pink toaster cakes with no problem and carried them to the express checkout line. I was rummaging in my purse for my wallet when I heard the bubbly, unmistakably enthusiastic sound of Tally Janeway's laugh.

I turned to see Tally getting in line right behind me, flanked by fellow theater nuts Audriana Bingley and Buster Hallowell. Buster was telling a story using his whole body for emphasis, bending forward and waggling his hands wildly. He was wearing a stunning array of colors, starting with orange sneakers and topped resplendently with a fire-engine red beret. You had to be a certain kind of person to pull that look off. Buster *was* that person.

"So she's like, 'Bees! I'm covered in bees!' And she's swatting at them, and her voice is getting higher and higher, and she just keeps repeating, 'Bees! I'm covered in beeeeeeeeees!'"

Tally was bent over laughing. I had no idea what Buster was talking about, but I started laughing, too. He was just too funny.

"But the thing is, it was actually only, like, three bees. And none of them stung her—I think they were just trying to be, like, *friendly* or something. But she just kept saying, 'Bees—'"

"'I'm covered in bees!'" Tally finished. She finally noticed me, standing there laughing along with them. "Hey, Paulina."

"Oh, strawberry Pop-Tarts," Audriana said, pointing at the box in my hand. "I love those."

"So do beeeeees," added Buster, cracking himself up again.

"Hey, guys," I said. They were like a traveling variety show when they hung out together.

"You should do food reviews for your magazine," Audriana said. "Then they'd have to give them to you for free. I totally want to work on a magazine someday. It sounds so glamorous."

Audriana was very short and had a pleasantly round face. Today she was favoring the thrift-shop military look, with camouflage pants and a black T-shirt.

"Speaking of which, are you psyched about the show?" I asked Tally.

"What show?" she asked

"The one you're going to write about," I said. "With the girl? Doing the accent? I thought you were going tonight."

Tally's mouth dropped open, and she slapped her hand over her forehead. "I forgot to buy a ticket," she said, grimacing.

"For what?" Audriana asked.

"Are we talking about *The Secret Garden*?" Buster chimed in. "I thought we were all going together for the final performance."

"I've got to go *tonight*!" Tally groaned.

"Opening night? You'll never get a ticket now," Audriana said.

"I *have* to get a ticket," Tally said. "Y'all, help me. Who can we call? Paulina," she said, turning to me. "Do not freak out, okay? I swear I will see the show and interview Devon and get the piece written by . . ."

"First draft Monday, final by Friday?" I offered.

Tally gulped, then nodded. "Absolutely no problem whatsoever," she said. "I promise."

"Bees," Buster started singing again. "I'm covered in bees . . ."

I was at the head of the line. I handed the cashier my Pop-Tarts. She was watching Buster with a tired expression her face.

I pocketed my change. "I'm sure it will be fine," I told

Tally. "No worries."

"Absolutely! No worries!" Tally declared, making a face that indicated there might actually be more than quite a few worries. But there was nothing I could do about it. Either Tally got herself to the play, or not.

"See you all later," I said.

I went out the exit that led directly outside. I didn't want to risk running into Alara in the mall. I had an unsettled feeling in my stomach for reasons I couldn't pinpoint—just a mixed bag of nervousness about the magazine, maybe, and basic anxiety about seventh grade, definitely. I really wanted to avoid tangling with Alara. I was never going to manage to smile at Benny Novak. I had a sort-of new friend, but the PQuits couldn't stand her, which meant they might decide to hate me, too.

But I also had a new outfit and had spent a great afternoon with Ivy. I had run into Benny Novak without embarrassment. And it was a Friday night, with the first hint of fall in the air. Maybe everything would work out A-OK after all.

I suddenly had a craving for a strawberry Pop-Tart. I ripped open the box and broke a bite-sized piece off. The jam and sugary pastry were delicious, and my day, for the time being, seemed perfectly complete.

· chapter ·

9

On Sunday night, I was curled up comfortably on my bed, trying to place a video call to Evelyn. My homework was done, and I was mostly through a first draft of the cyberbullying article. I was ready for a break and eager to talk to my best friend. I had opened my Skype account and was figuring out where I was supposed to type in Evelyn's address when I noticed a new message in my in-box. I clicked on it.

▼ **To:** Paulina M. Barbosa
▼ **From:** Fashion Maven
Subject: Magazine piece and blog

The blog is set up. Click on the link at the bottom of my e-mail to view. I sent the link to some people and asked them to forward it to their friends. We still need a name for the magazine. Since we're writing the magazine and blog for girls, and we also happen to be four girls, what about the title *4 Girls*?

Also, I'm submitting a poem for my text contribution to the magazine. It's attached as a Word doc. Paulina, since you're the editor, you can let me know if it needs work. I'll make changes or write something different if you want. But if you use the poem, my name does not go on it. It has to be anonymous, or it's a no go.

I definitely would not have figured Miko for the poetry type. Curious to see what she had come up with, I opened the attachment.

Shinto

This face is not me.
This voice, not me.
What you see is what you do not get.
My true self cannot be seen.

I am more than what you think.
Less than what you know.
Deeper than you can imagine.
More insignificant than you dream.

How do I tell you?

I am the mountains.
The river.
The rocks.
The sea.

You are the mountains.
The river.
The rocks.
The sea.

Are we so different,
you and I?
We are lit within by the same star.
A divine spark of light.

Do you see?

We are the mystery.
The green book of life.
So old.
So bright.

I took a deep breath. Miko had written this? Was she talking about herself—telling the world she wanted to be seen as she really was? But her e-mail said she didn't want her name published with the poem. Why would someone write such a beautiful message about who they were deep inside but refuse to include their name?

Maybe it is because of the PQuits, I thought. I could imagine them ridiculing a poem like this. Which might explain a thing or two about Miko—maybe her creative side and her social side were trying to cancel each other out.

I read the poem again, savoring the last lines . . . *the*

green book of life. So old. So bright. I loved the image. It seemed so hopeful, and the mystery of it gave me goose bumps. And I felt like I knew exactly what she was trying to say about being more than she seemed on the surface. I felt that way about myself sometimes.

I noticed Miko had only sent the poem to me.

Well, I was the editor. So it was my job to do first read-throughs and give feedback. *Don't overthink this,* I told myself. *Just respond.*

▼ **To:** Fashion Maven
▼ **From:** Paulina M. Barbosa
Subject: Re: Magazine piece and blog

Thanks for setting up the blog. I love the idea of *4 Girls* and the pun on *for* and *four* girls. Let's run it by the others.

Also, I think the poem is really good. There's not really anything I think you need to change. Do you mind my asking what *Shinto* means? Readers might wonder that, too. I guess it's not a problem to publish it without your name, but are you sure? If I had written something that good, I'd want my name on it.

I hit Send quickly, so I couldn't second-guess suggesting changes just to feel like an editor. I stared at the screen, then I went to the blog link Miko had sent.

The home page for the blog was cute—speckled with little suns and moons and a single star from which swung the figure of a girl. The background was a deep sky-blue, and the text a summer grass-green.

Blogpost: Welcome!
Posted by: 4Girls

Welcome to the blog for the upcoming Bixby Middle School magazine, written by girls, for girls. Our first issue will be out at the end of September.

The purpose of this blog is to give everyone a voice and a safe place to speak. Anyone who wants to talk about something, whether it's a TV show or a big life issue, is welcome here. Two rules: No real names and no judging. Trolls are *not* welcome. If you want to post something mean, find another site.

It looked good. Did it need more direction, though? Maybe there was an issue I should suggest we discuss. It would be lame to have a blog up there with absolutely nothing on it.

Could I do something like that without checking with the others first?

I was trying to come up with a good topic when my Skype screen began blinking, accompanied by an electronic ringing noise. I clicked the button that said ANSWER VIDEO CALL and was delighted and amazed to see Evelyn's familiar, freckled face appear on my screen. She was leaning forward and squinting at the keyboard.

"Why isn't this stupid thing working?" she muttered.

"It is working!" I cried. "Ev, do you see me?"

Evelyn jumped back a little like the keyboard had bit her. Then her face broke into a wide smile, displaying the little gap between her front teeth that she hated.

"Paulie," she said. "This is awesome. Can you hear me okay? Are you in your room? I recognize the quilt on the bed. I miss your room! Mine is freezing."

"I miss you being in my room," I said. "So how is everything?"

Evelyn rolled her eyes and ran one hand through her short, red-gold hair.

"School is crazy," she said. "It's like twenty times the size of Bixby. I practically need a topographical map and a compass just to find my way to class. But my math teacher is a dead ringer for Agent Booth from *Bones* which is so thoroughly motivating."

I laughed.

"Well, Bixby is as small as ever, but it's crazy, too. One week in, and the homework is piling on, plus I've got this CEP thing to do and only two weeks left till the deadline. We are starting a blog, too!"

Evelyn's eyebrows shot up.

"Really? That's cool. So is Miko Suzuki really in on this project, or were you just joking with me?"

"No, she is," I said. "There are four of us. Me, Miko, Tally Janeway, and a new girl, Ivy Scanlon, who is actually really cool. She's from New York City, and she wears these vintage clothes that are amazing. We went to the mall together on Friday and had cappuccinos, and she found this great outfit for me at H&M for practically nothing. I'll take a picture of me wearing it and send it to you."

"Since when do you drink cappuccino?" Evelyn asked. Her forehead wrinkled as she peered out at me.

I shrugged. "Since Friday, I guess. Ivy is all about coffee. She lives in that big, old, stone farmhouse you pass on the way to the Ski Barn. Remember it? She said she's going to have me over, and I can't wait to finally see what it looks like on the inside. Oh, and Ivy's mother used to be the editor in chief of *City Nation*. How amazing is that?"

Evelyn frowned slightly.

"Sounds like you're getting along just fine without me," she said.

Oops. I knew that look. The last thing Evelyn needed to think was that I'd already replaced her.

"It's just that I've seen a lot of her because of the magazine," I said quickly. "She's the only one I can really work with because Tally is as insane as ever. She claims she was bitten by a vampire bat in the music room! She keeps asking people to look at her teeth because she's convinced she's growing fangs. And Miko hates Ivy. All the PQuits do."

I almost added the part about Ivy giving Shelby the brush-off when they met, but decided I should probably ease up on the Ivy talk for a while.

"So Miko Suzuki is actually doing this project?" Evelyn asked. "I cannot picture it!"

She started to laugh and leaned forward, so all I could see was a blurry close-up of the top of her head.

"Yes!" I said. "She's doing all the layout and design work, at least we hope she is, and she also just sent me a—"

I cut myself off before saying anything about the poem.

"She sent you a what?" Evelyn asked, sitting back and coming into focus on my screen again.

Could I say something about the poem? Evelyn wasn't even at Bixby anymore, so what harm was there? It wasn't like I was Miko's friend.

But I am her editor, I thought. *And she trusted me with that poem.*

"She sent me a link to our blog," I said. "There's nothing on it yet, but hopefully there will be soon. There are three other groups competing with us, and one of them is a softball team. Alara Jameson is in that group!"

"Ooooh, be careful," Evelyn said. "Alara, Alara, Alara the Hun—she'll smite you with her bully's breath . . ."

"And eat you when she's done!" I finished. "I know. I've managed to avoid a run-in so far, but that can't last forever. She'll probably find out about the blog soon, too. You know how she loves torturing people over the Internet."

"She'll be all over that blog. I can't wait to see it," Evelyn declared, grinning. "I can imagine the flame wars right now—Jocks dumping on Computer Nerds and PQuits piling on Brains . . ."

"But that's exactly what we *don't* want," I said. "The whole point is to have a place where you can post your thoughts without attaching your name and have people really respond to you without worrying about how they're supposed to be treating you or what their friends would think. Think how amazing it could be, Ev. Like, what if when my parents split, I could have written about it and heard back from other girls at school who went through the same thing or had some advice. People I never would have confided in or even talked to otherwise. Maybe even a PQuit would end up being really kind or supportive. They'd just be posting with some screen name. A PQuit on the outside could be a totally different person on the inside, and we'd never know it!"

Evelyn stared at me for a moment. Then she cracked up.

"Yup, you're probably right," she said. "I'm sure all the PQuits are secretly deep, compassionate, and enlightened beings."

"Well, I'm just saying it's possible."

"Of course it's *possible*," Evelyn said. "And when we sign off, it is possible I'm going to grow wings and fly around my room for a while."

"Let me know how that works out for you," I said, then I sighed. I wished Evelyn were still at Bixby and could see my group in action. Maybe then it wouldn't be so hard to believe what was possible.

"Oh, and my mother has officially gone insane," Evelyn said, leaning forward and lowering her voice. "You would not believe the situation we had the other day."

"I'm all ears," I said.

The little e-mail symbol in my toolbar lit up. As Evelyn began outlining her mother's outrageous position on appropriate footwear, I opened my in-box. There was an automated e-mail telling me that the blog had been updated.

Our first post!

Apparently I could pull whatever I wanted up on my screen, and my video image was still being sent to Evelyn. I was listening to my friend's story. I really was. But I also could not resist checking out our very first blog entry.

Blogpost: I Hate Haters
Posted by: LowdMusikGurrl

I know this is seventh grade and everything, but has anyone else noticed that people at school seem to be acting especially jerky lately? I was in the cafeteria Friday trying to eat in peace, and the amount of trashing and ragging on people I overheard was completely insane. I heard people trashed for their looks, their clothes, their weight, and their friends. One kid was making fun of some girl whose house got painted a supposedly ugly color this summer.

Sometimes I feel like I just can't deal with the haters anymore. It's too much—there's mean stuff everywhere. I'm so tired of it—even when it isn't directed at me. Don't we all have enough to worry about? Between grades and teachers and parents and everything . . . my grandfather had a heart attack last week. It's scary. Everyone's freaked out at my house. And then I come to school, and all I hear is people being nasty. It's just really depressing to me.

So I'm just curious, I guess. Is it me, am I just totally oversensitive, or is there just a lot more mindless girl-bashing-girl stuff going on?

Anyway. Love the blog, can't wait for the magazine.

"Which is absolutely certifiable," Evelyn was saying. "I mean, who is even wearing Crocs anymore? So the tragedy of pink Crocs? I can't even tell you."

I pushed the button that would maximize Evelyn's image back to full screen. I was really excited about the first blog entry, but there was no way to say so without clueing Evelyn in on my . . . well, multitasking.

"Pink Crocs certainly seem cruel and unusual," I said.

"Exactly!" Evelyn cried. "But my mother thinks they're adorable—that's the word she keeps using. Adorable to who?"

"You could—"

Evelyn shot a hand up in a traffic cop "stop" gesture, turning around to face in the opposite direction.

"Paulie, I gotta go," Evelyn said. "She's wandering around near my door, and she doesn't know I'm Skyping with you. She has this ridiculous rule that I'm not allowed to put my picture anywhere on the Internet, and I don't want her to see I'm using the webcam and get all freaked out."

"No problem," I said. "Why don't we—"

I could see the door behind Evelyn begin to open as she reached out and snapped her laptop closed. My screen went black.

"Talk tomorrow," I finished. "Oh well."

I went back to the blog. There was already a response posted. I couldn't believe it!

Re: Blogpost: I Hate Haters
Posted by: HobbitFan

It's not just you. I am definitely experiencing the mean. The only thing I can say is that we can each make a choice not to participate. It might not seem like much, but if even five people decide to lay off the gossip and griping for a while, it will make a difference.

And I'm really sorry about your grandfather. If it helps, my dad had a heart attack last year, and he's fine now. His doctor actually said the heart attack was kind of a good thing because it caused him to find out there was a problem and change his eating habits to get healthier. So hopefully your grandfather will be okay, too!

That's really nice, I thought. *That girl is going to read this and probably feel better.*

Writing a proposal about doing something to make a difference was one thing. So was talking about it. But now I was looking at something actually happening. The blog hadn't been up for more than an hour or two, and one person had already provided a little support to another girl. And neither of them even knew the other one's name.

I sat back and stared at the screen. I'd been planning to curl up with a book after talking to Evelyn. But now I was thinking about my article on cyberbullying. It was a decent draft. But could I make it better? Seeing LowdMusikGurrl's and HobbitFan's posts had suddenly made the hazy idea of readers extremely real to me.

I sent a quick e-mail to Ivy and Tally asking them what they thought of the name *4 Girls*.

Then I pulled up my article and began to type.

· chapter ·

10

I was on a search and retrieve mission in my least favorite place—the cafeteria. Tuesday was chicken fried rice day for those who bought their lunch, and the smell was overpowering. But after I got Ivy's latest e-mail, there was just no way to avoid it. I had to find Tally and Miko right away.

▼ **To:** Paulina M. Barbosa
▼ **From:** IvyNYC
Subject: Re: Cover?

You are totally right. I can't BELIEVE I didn't think of this. Yes, we do have to come up with a separate topic to feature on the cover. The notes about your cyberbullying article look great, but it doesn't feel like cover material to me. I think our first issue needs to feature something specifically from school, not an issue. Do you agree? My article isn't right for the cover, either—it's about that singer who went here (Esme Stand) and how she ended up as a successful indie artist, plus I did a review of her latest album. I don't know if Tally has even started her thing on the play—she hasn't answered my last two e-mails. We were sort of on schedule before, but this is a lot of new work that blows the whole process out of the water. We need an emergency meeting! Can you find Tally and Miko at lunchtime? Mrs. Finley came through with the spare office for us to use—I will run and get the key and meet you guys there—room 107.

Also, yes, I'm liking the sound of *4 Girls.* Bet you came up with it, right?

I found Miko first, sitting at the PQuit table with Shelby Simpson and Claudia Dickerson. Shelby saw me approaching the table, and she wrinkled her nose.

"Those seats are taken," Shelby said, indicating the two empty chairs. "Daphne and Charelle sit there."

"I know that," I said, irritated. Like I would suddenly decide I wanted to eat lunch with the PQuits? Like I didn't know how the world worked?

"Miko, I'm really sorry, but we're having an emergency CEP meeting right now," I said. "Can you come? We've only got what's left of this period."

"She's eating her lunch," Shelby said. Miko's lunch was unpacked and laid out on the table. An avocado roll and mineral water. Even her lunch looked too cool for me.

"I'm really sorry, Miko," I repeated. "You can bring your lunch with you. We just kind of have a problem we need to deal with right away."

"What problem?" Miko asked.

"Ivy e-mailed you—it's about the—"

"Ivy?" Shelby said, making a face. "That girl is bad news. Nobody likes her. I heard she got busted for stealing at her old school, and—"

"Miko, please," I said more loudly. "We really need you."

I felt a little bad for Miko because she looked genuinely embarrassed. I hadn't been able to think of her the same way since reading her poem. She now seemed like a person being pulled in two opposite directions, and I wasn't doing her any favors by reminding Shelby that Ivy was part of the CEP group. I honestly expected her to flat-out refuse to come.

"Whatever," Shelby said. "You should have planned ahead."

But Miko put her avocado roll into a plastic bag.

"Fine," she said.

She didn't look happy, but she stood up, ready to come work with the group.

"Room 107," I said. "Mrs. Finley is letting us use it. I've still got to find Tally. I'll meet you there?"

"Fine," Miko repeated. "Shel, I'll catch you in English. Don't forget to bring me that note!"

Miko swept out of the cafeteria as fast as she could. It was fine. I didn't want to walk with her any more than she did with me. Plus, I had to track Tally down.

I found Tally down the hall by the water fountain, riffling through her book bag. When she saw me, she grabbed my arm.

"Please tell me you went to social studies and took amazing notes and that you'll let me look at them so I don't flunk this test on Friday and get executed by Ms. Zootsuit," Tally begged, fixing me with a pleading stare.

"We have to go to a meeting," I told her. "Right now. It's an emergency."

Tally's eyes got huge. "Have there been more sightings? Are they nearby?"

"We . . . what?" I asked.

Tally stuffed her things back in her book bag and tried to yank the zipper closed.

"It's been happening all week," she said. "Scarsdale, El Paso, and Saint Paul. Those were the first three."

"The first three what?" I asked. "And can you just walk with me while you answer that? We really have to go."

Tally gave up on the zipper and held the book bag in her arms like a baby.

"I know we do!" she said. "I mean, we don't even know if they're friendly. We don't even know what they want!"

I picked up the pace, and Tally trotted beside me, her curls bouncing wildly.

"What are you talking about, Tally?"

"The UFO sightings," Tally exclaimed. "Did you see the video they had on the news last night? I don't care who you are, nobody can explain away three identical, V-shaped light formations that hover in one place for twenty minutes in three separate places across the country. Y'all, they're here! So where does the government say we should go? The gymnasium? A safe house?"

"Tally, we're having an emergency CEP meeting," I said. "In room 107. That's what I've been trying to tell you. For the *4 Girls* cover situation."

"What's *4 Girls*?" Tally asked.

How did Tally even manage to find the floor with her feet when she got up in the morning?

"It's the name of our magazine," I said. "Didn't you read my e-mail? How it seemed catchy since the magazine is for girls and it's created by four girls?"

"And we're the four?" Tally asked.

"Yes, Tally," I said, with what I thought was mind-blowing patience. "We are the four."

"I like it," Tally said.

"Great. Then it's unanimous. This meeting is because we have to come up with a cover article."

"I totally agree! We can list all the cities that have been visited so far and talk about what technology they might have, and what to do if the aliens approach us personally because really we're all ambassadors to our planet now and—"

"We're not doing a cover article on UFO sightings," I said. Was Tally for real? I had never encountered anyone who seemed to operate so far from reality.

"Why not?" Tally asked. "What else are people going to want to read about?"

"Did you finish your review of the play?" I asked. "You didn't e-mail any notes. I've got to have it, Tally. It needs to be in and final by Friday."

Tally fell silent. For once she suddenly seemed to have absolutely nothing to say.

"At least tell me you've started it," I said.

Tally was avoiding my gaze, checking doors left and right.

"Room 107, you said?" she asked. "I think this might be it."

"Tally, please tell me you've started your article," I repeated gently.

Tally came to a sudden halt and stared at me, eyes saucer shaped, like she'd just caught sight of one of those UFOs she kept talking about. I began to get a very bad feeling.

"You did go to see the play, right?" I asked.

Tally wilted like a flower in the sun. "I couldn't get a ticket," she whispered.

I groaned.

Tally quickly opened the door to room 107 and slipped inside.

Miko and Ivy were sitting at a small, round table. The room was spacious and sunny and had a large desk and computer, a bookshelf, and a slightly droopy plant. They both looked at me expectantly. I almost blurted out the news that Tally had missed the play but decided to wait for her to tell them herself.

"I know we don't have a lot of time," I said, pulling up a chair.

"Right," Ivy said. "So as Paulina so brilliantly pointed out to me in an e-mail last night, we're missing something big. In addition to the individual articles we're each doing, we need to agree on a cover topic— something that every girl at school knows about and has an opinion on—and we need to get that article researched and written. Like, yesterday."

"Are you serious?" Miko asked. "I need time to do the layout, and I can't do it if all the writing isn't finished. How will I know how much space to leave for each piece? I've also got to finish work on the logo. If you're saying there's going to be another whole article and it's going to affect what goes on the cover, that's a big problem for me."

"It's a problem for *all* of us," Ivy said. "We're just going to have to work harder and faster to make sure we get it all done."

"In case you haven't noticed, there is a social studies exam scheduled for Friday, a bio exam on Monday, a book report due a few days after that, and they're starting a special study session for the state math test, which I have to go to," Miko said. She glared at Ivy.

"I have noticed," Ivy said coolly. "I've also noticed that Pitch In has gotten over two hundred signatures on their petition, they have a website, and they're almost finished with a video about the team to post on it."

"And the fourth group is pitching a student book club, and they've already come up with a schedule of titles, and they've contacted two authors they might be able to bring in for visits," I added.

"I know all of that," Miko said, still scowling. "And what I'm saying to you is I don't know where these extra hours are supposed to come from. I was supposed to have all the articles in final form with whatever photos you wanted to go with them. I have Ivy's, and Paulina said she could e-mail hers to me by Friday—"

"Which I will," I said.

"And I need Tally's, which I don't even have a rough word count for, and that gives me enough time to get my layout done by Monday morning if I work nonstop. Ivy said she has to have the DVD with the file on it to bring to the printers that day. I have to start going to math prep sessions this week. There's just not enough time to add on one more thing."

"But we have to make the time," Ivy said. "Look, I have the same workload as you, and I know it's crazy, but this magazine is really important to me."

Miko rolled her eyes. "And it isn't important to the rest of us? We're all just here to make things easier for you?"

"I didn't say that," Ivy said quietly.

"It's exactly what you said," Miko snapped. "You have no idea the kind of pressure I'm under right now. None of you do! Don't put this all on me."

She looked like she was going to storm out of the room right then.

I thought of her poem. *Are we so different, you and I?*

"Look," I said suddenly. "I think all we have to do right now is agree to keep trying. I mean, if that's what we're all willing to do."

All three of them looked at me, and nobody said anything. I decided to take that as a yes.

"I'm still on target to finish my article by Friday," I said. "And so far I'm really happy with it. I found this organization online that has a forum for issues of cyberbullying, and there's some really interesting stuff there. I can also take some extra time to make some lists of possible cover topics. Miko's already finished her . . . contribution. Which I have. And, Ivy, things sound like they're going smoothly with your article and review of Esme Stand and the new CD."

"She responded to my e-mail, actually," Ivy said. "So I'm going to have a few quotes from her that are directly addressed to Bixby girls."

"Fabulous!" I said. I looked around at everyone, silently urging them to agree with me. I caught Miko's eye. She started to look away, then looked back at me. Her expression softened, and she gave me a small, almost imperceptible nod.

I felt a wave of relief because at that moment I knew that if Miko decided to abandon ship, Tally would quickly follow, and we'd be sunk. I gave Miko my most reassuring, supportive smile.

"What about you, Tally?" Miko said. "Do you have photos of the play you're going to want run? Or will we just have one of Devon?"

Tally pitched herself forward and thunked her head onto the table. Then she lifted it slightly and did it again. *Thunk.*

Thunk.

Thunk.

"Okay, that is giving me a bad feeling," Ivy said. "What is it? Was the play so awful you can't think of a way to give it a positive spin?"

Tally raised her head slightly. "I haven't seen it," she said.

"What?" Miko exclaimed.

"I couldn't get a ticket!" Tally wailed.

"Tally, you were supposed to go last Friday," Ivy said. "Today is Tuesday. When were you thinking of mentioning this?"

"I was going to!" Tally said. "But over the weekend I was online and that's when I heard about the UFOs, and I worried myself into a pickle about it all weekend and couldn't sleep, which is why I missed social studies this morning, because I was having a flat-out panic attack, and I know the best thing to do is just carry on and breathe because they might just be observing us and not planning on invading the planet at all, but I've still missed the show now, and they don't have another performance until Friday night, which is after the article is due, so I can't possibly write the review unless I make it up, which is a total no-no in the theater, though, if you really thought I should—"

"Tal, stop!" Miko interrupted.

"Seriously," muttered Ivy.

Tally fixed each of them with an imploring look, in quick succession.

"Okay, so you missed the play. Why not just come up with a different idea to write about?" Miko asked.

Tally's mouth dropped open. "I can do that?"

"Of course you can," Ivy said. "That's part of the whole process. Ideas get scrapped for whatever reason. New ones replace them. As long as you write something that relates to our readers, what difference does it make?"

"But . . . I don't have a different idea," Tally said. "I don't have anything to say."

"Of course you do," Miko said. "What about the pressure of memorizing lines when you've got homework to do? Or what about that thing you were saying to Daphne yesterday about how when you get to middle school it seems like you're supposed to choose between being cool and getting good grades?"

"Either of those sound like they have potential," Ivy said. She gave Tally an encouraging smile.

"They do?" Tally asked, looking amazed.

"They absolutely do," I agreed. "You just have to promise to get to work on one of them and not stop till it's done."

Tally clasped her hands in front of her heart, reminding me of a blond, neurotic Dorothy from *The Wizard of Oz*.

"Oh, y'all, I *do* promise," she declared. "Nothing, I mean nothing, will stop me from getting this done.

Even if I have to e-mail it to you from the dungeon on an alien planet, I will!"

"But do alien dungeons have Wi-Fi?" I asked.

Ivy laughed as the bell rang.

"We're all going to be late for next period," Miko said, standing up hastily.

"You're right," I said. "We better go. So we're all okay?"

"Better than okay," Tally proclaimed. "I feel like I've been given a second chance at *life*!"

"I'll just stick with okay," Ivy said.

"Yeah, we're good," Miko added, looking only at me. "Later."

She headed out the door, Tally bouncing behind her like a bunny on caffeine. Ivy stood up and pulled the strap of her messenger bag over her shoulder.

"You have the patience of a saint with both of them," Ivy said. "I was about to lose my temper and start yelling. I guess Tally means well, but she's, like, the perfect storm or something. And Miko is such a princess I can barely keep from reaching over and smacking her in the head. That girl really rubs me the wrong way."

"I don't know," I said as we walked out of the room. "I think there actually may be more to Miko than we think."

"More layers of fluff and entitlement, you mean?" Ivy said.

"No, seriously. She wrote a poem for the magazine. She sent it to me."

"Let me guess," Ivy said, grinning. "Roses are red, violets are blue, because I'm a PQuit, I'm better than you."

"Um, no," I said, laughing. "I can send it to you. We should all probably read over one another's stuff and okay it before we decide it's final."

"Definitely send me Miko's 'poem,'" Ivy said. "This, I cannot wait to see."

Ivy was heading to the new wing of the school, and I had to get up to the second floor, so our conversation was cut short. I would e-mail Ivy Miko's poem later—maybe it would speak for itself.

And I couldn't wait to Skype Evelyn and tell her about the impending alien invasion.

Though I knew she would find that more believable than my budding acceptance, and possibly even a tiny bit of admiration, for Miko Suzuki.

· chapter ·
11

I surprised myself by finishing my article during last period study hall on Thursday afternoon. An entire day ahead of schedule. I'd type up the edits, and I could e-mail it to Miko tonight. Then I could get back to sifting through ideas for the cover article.

I was still shoving things in my book bag as I headed down the hall toward the main exit. My mother worked late on Thursdays, so if I missed the bus I was up a creek without a paddle, and so, by extension, was my little brother.

"Social studies textbook," I said out loud to myself, checking to make sure it was in my bag. "And the study outline for the next test," I added, pulling three pieces of paper in and out before finding the right one.

I reminded myself (yes, out loud) that I also needed the paperback math workbook that had a website address for the state math exam practice tests.

"No, the blue cover. The one with the blue cover," I scolded my hand, which had retrieved a book with a red cover and a picture of a volcano on the front.

"Who are you talking to?"

The voice startled me, and I dropped my bag on the floor. Busted. And by the worst person possible.

Alara Jameson.

"Nobody," I said.

I quickly retrieved my bag and shoved everything inside. Then I made a move to go around Alara, but she stepped into my path. She was carrying a duffel bag that smelled like old shoes and from which the ends of two softball bats protruded.

"Running to one of your little magazine meetings?" Alara asked. "Don't bother. There's no way you're going to beat Pitch In."

I shrugged. "I guess we'll see," I said quietly. "They're both good causes."

"A girls' magazine," Alara said in a singsong voice. "So *precious*. So very honor roll of you. You guys are a total joke. You realize that, right?"

Last year, any kind of run-in with Alara had really upset me. And I wasn't exactly enjoying myself right now. But now Alara felt like a big irritation instead of a scary intimidation. A fat mosquito buzzing insistently around my head.

"Whatever," I told Alara, trying to go around her. This time she simply started walking next to me.

"Word is you guys are behind schedule, can't agree on anything, and don't even really like one another," Alara said. "What's left, like a week for you to finish and hand something out? You might as well give up now. You guys are flying blind. You're total amateurs who have no idea what you're doing. You've done, like, nothing."

"We haven't done *nothing*," I blurted out. "We've got articles, interviews, a layout—we even have a blog. And people are already posting on it—they love it! And we're not amateurs, either. Ivy's mother used to be a big-time editor at *City Nation* magazine. She knows more about how to do this than anyone— even down to where to get software for the layout. We are more in the game than you'll ever be. I'll put my money on our magazine over a group of girls throwing a ball around any day."

Alara came to a sudden stop in front of me, sticking out her hand.

"Are you talking about me? And my team?" she demanded.

"I'm talking about any team," I said. "At the end of the day, you're just playing a game. We're using our brains and doing something really valuable to change the world."

Alara's face had gone red. "Oh, so if you're smarter than me, you're a more valuable person?" she asked.

"I don't know, Alara. That's what you seem to think. I mean, why else would you stay mad for three years because you said something stupid in science?"

"I am *not* stupid!" Alara snapped.

I should have told Alara that of course she was not stupid, that nobody thought that. But instead, I just shrugged.

Alara's face went from red to purple, and I knew I should have kept my mouth shut. What I really meant was that my problem with Alara was her being mean, not whether she was a rocket scientist. But now I was the one saying nasty things.

I could see my bus through the glass door, and everyone else had already gotten on. Alara looked so enraged I thought she might actually haul off and hit me. I decided I should get out of there fast.

I pushed past Alara, through the door, and was on the bus just as the doors were about to close.

I've got to tell Evelyn about this, I thought.

But as I ran the encounter over in my head, practicing how I would relate it to my friend, nothing I'd said sounded clever. I really didn't want to tell anyone, even Evelyn, that I'd shown Alara up by being snarky to her. In fact, the whole thing had left a bad taste in my mouth.

I got out my iPod and tried to enjoy the ten-minute bus ride as kind of forced relaxation. I had a lot of studying to do after getting my article off to Miko. Plus, I was in charge of dinner again, and chances were good Kevin would need to be walked through his math homework. My iPod froze, though, and between that and the bus driver actively seeking out and hitting every pothole on the road, I was feeling even more upset when I got home.

I pushed through the front door and took a deep, calming breath. Kevin was getting a ride home from his friend's mom, so I had about an hour of quiet. I ran upstairs, grabbed my laptop, and brought it down to the kitchen. I set it on the counter, where I found a note from my mother asking me to defrost a casserole she'd left in the freezer. I pulled the casserole out and left it on the counter. Then I pulled my assignment pad from my book bag and flipped through the pages, noticing with a groan I'd forgotten I had a book report coming up for English.

When had life gotten this crazy and complicated?

"I thought these were supposed to be the best years of my life," I muttered. "Okay, just relax and focus. One thing at a time. The article."

I pulled out my notes and opened the file. Then I started to type.

We live in a world our mothers probably never dreamed of when they were kids. Could anyone have ever imagined there would be something like the Internet or cell phones? Facebook or Twitter? We can be in touch with one another almost anytime we want. We can store our pictures, our videos, and our memories so that they can never get lost or damaged. Our parents feel comfortable giving us more freedom because with a cell phone we're never farther than a phone call or a text message away. All this technology connects us and gives us the opportunity to stay in touch, to reach out, and to be closer to our friends and family than any generation before us. All these wonderful inventions, from e-mail to smartphones, have the potential to build us up.

Unless they tear us down first.

It's called cyberbullying—using electronic technology to harass another person. Some studies show that 20 percent of all people will experience cyberbullying by the time they are eighteen years old. And girls are more likely to be cyberbullied than boys. All these new technologies and social networks have the potential to make the problem much, much worse. How many of you have ever texted something mean about somebody? Left a rude comment on someone's Facebook wall? Forwarded somebody an e-mail that wasn't meant for them to read? Guess what—that all falls under the definition of cyberbullying. In some forms it's just a pesky irritation. But there are times when cyberbullying can harm a person, creating enormous personal pain or even an emotional breakdown.

It's so easy to start a rumor on the Internet. Push a few buttons, and there it is. It basically spreads by itself. Once something is out there, it's really hard for anybody to know where it came from or whether it's true. A rumor takes on a life of its own, whether you mean it to or not. And who really cares? You don't even have to put your real name. Nobody will even know it was you, so it's not your problem, is it? A little harmless gossip isn't cyberbullying, right?

Wrong. Very, very wrong.

When you text or post on Facebook about someone or you send around a stupid picture or an e-mail that wasn't meant for other people's eyes, it's out there forever. You might delete it or try to take it back or take it off your wall. But chances are somebody will have already seen it, and if they didn't see it, they will talk to someone who did. In other words, it's getting much easier for us to cause embarrassment, or actual hurt, for one another. Now more than ever, we have to be careful about what we say and how we say it. The technology is always changing, and we have to start changing with it.

As many as two-thirds of all students our age go online every day to connect with one another or do schoolwork. That's a huge explosion in the online population, and the increase in cyberbullying attacks has come right along with it. Because it's hard to trace the source, and because the use of words or pictures to bully is sometimes seen as less "serious" than physical violence, schools, parents, and even the police aren't in agreement over when and how to take measures to stop it. The burden is going to fall on us to educate ourselves and develop a sense of responsibility about this issue.

My suggestion for one way to do this is simple: Never text or post anything you wouldn't say or do in person. Respect the power of the written word. Don't say something you might never be able to take back. And remember that something that might seem like a little harmless pranking to you might be devastating to someone else.

It's an amazing time to be in the world. We

can communicate over any distance practically through thin air. Let's just make sure that in the process, we never lose sight of one another.

I reread the article twice.

There was a lot more I could say—more statistics I could include or real-life cyberbullying horror stories I could recount. But I didn't want to sound preachy or dry. If I wanted other girls to relate to my point, I needed to sound like one of them, not like a public service announcement.

I decided to leave the article as it was and sent it to Miko before I could change my mind and start fiddling with it again.

I had just started an outline for my book report when the front door flew open with a bang. Moments later, Kevin skidded into the kitchen in his socks, shoes in one hand. We were a no-shoes house, and it was the only rule Kevin seemed to remember on a regular basis.

"It's starting to get cool out there. If your toes freeze, do they fall off? Are you making dinner? Luke says there's going to be a fight at school. My English teacher told us you're writing a book about kids. Am I in it? Do you think Mom will let us get a cat?"

Kevin paused to take a breath.

"Hi, Kevin. My day was fine. How was yours?"

Kevin opened the refrigerator and stared inside it.

"I got an eighty on my math quiz. Douglas found a slug in his lunch box, and he ate it," he said. "Do you think he's going to die?"

"That's fabulous!" I said. "The eighty in math, I mean, not the slug. I somehow doubt he really ate it, Kev. And no, I'm not writing a book. There are four girls putting together a magazine. I'm one of the four—I told you about it, remember? We're trying to win money for a new school club. Although at this point I have so much homework backed up, I don't even know if I can pass some of my classes, let alone get the magazine done. You'll see what I mean when you get to middle school next year. They really pile on the work."

"I don't want to go to middle school," Kevin said. "Anyway, I might not have to. Luke said we're probably getting invaded by UFOs, but hopefully not till after Christmas, so we'll still get our presents. If aliens end up running the earth, we won't have to go to school. I'm not scared of them, though."

Kevin closed the refrigerator door, and his voice trailed off. He actually did look a little alarmed. An alien invasion? Where did Luke get his news?

Probably the same place Tally does, I thought.

"There aren't any aliens, and no one is invading the planet," I told Kevin. "Which is a good thing for

118

them because they'd be no match for you and your laser when it's set on stun."

"Phasers get set on stun, not lasers," Kevin corrected.

"Phasers, right," I said. "From *Star Wars*."

"*Star Trek*," he corrected. "*Star Wars* has lightsabers."

"I get them both confused with *Stargate*," I said.

"*Stargate* has A'tar Blades, shock spears, M60s, Goa'uld Busters, the Rod of Anguish, and about a million other cool things," my brother lectured. "But no phasers, no lasers."

"I like the sound of those," I told him.

"Want to watch some episodes? I have the first season on DVD."

"I can't, Kev," I said. His face fell. Kevin was the only person I know who literally stuck out his lower lip when he was feeling sulky about something.

"I've got a ton of homework to do and dinner to heat up, and you have homework, too."

"Ewww, what is this?" He peered over the edge of the casserole dish, his nose pinched between two fingers.

"It's dinner, Kev. It's a . . . Mom said it's . . . casserole."

Kevin looked at me through sad, scared eyes. Rightfully so, I might add. My mother stuck all kinds of revolting things in casseroles and relied on soy cheese and heat to disguise them.

"It looks like space slugs in broccoli Jell-O," Kevin complained.

I got up and peeked into the casserole. I could not argue with his description. I wasn't sure my brain could withstand another long evening of doing my homework and helping with Kevin's, especially while powered by mystery casserole.

"Okay, listen. If you promise to start your homework right now—" I started.

Kevin instantly sprang to attention. "Yes!" he shouted.

"And . . . if you do what I say and are quiet when I'm doing my work—"

"Yes!" Kevin shouted again.

"Then I could probably accidentally forget this casserole was in the freezer and get us some dinner from Pizza Pete's."

"Sausage, pepperoni, ham, anchovies, extra onions!" Kevin exclaimed.

I pointed a finger at him. "Sit. Homework. Focus."

He grabbed his backpack from the floor and was seated at the kitchen table in an instant, the picture of angelic goodness.

I smiled. "Okay. I'll call in the order. But no anchovies."

Kevin knew enough to quit while he was ahead. And the pizza did, in fact, buy me a few hours of quiet study time. By the time Mom finally got home, at almost eight, we had both retreated to our rooms, having worked and eaten to the best of our abilities. I was considering sneaking down to the kitchen for a final cold slice when my cell phone rang.

It was Ivy. She cut right to the chase.

"Have you seen the blog tonight?"

"No. Why?" I asked.

"Just look," she said. "You'll know what I'm talking about as soon as you see it. Call me back."

She hung up without any further explanation.

I opened my laptop and clicked over to the blog. There were six new entries, but I immediately saw the one that had gotten Ivy's attention.

Blogpost: Is This Blog Run by Cheaters?
Posted by: Anonymous

Do you hate cheaters? If the answer is yes, read this! Everybody's heard about the CEP competition by now. (And if you haven't, crawl out from under that rock and talk to somebody.) There are four groups in the running—Pitch In for the softball team, a book club/author visit group, a sponsor-a-child overseas group, and a girls' magazine group—the same group that put up this blog. The rules are clear, stick to the budget and no outside financial or professional help.

The winner gets funding for their group.

So guess what? The four girls in the magazine group are CHEATING. One of their mothers is an editor at *City Nation*. She runs the magazine as her job. She's supervising everything this group does and giving them advice on how to win. She's also having her company do their design work for them. They can't stop bragging about how much more professional their project is than the other three. Well, why wouldn't it be? The professionals are doing it for them!

The other groups going for the funding are playing by the rules—by themselves. We're not taking anyone's secret money or getting some pro to do our thinking for us. But the four girls are.

THE FOUR SHOULD BE DISQUALIFIED! And next Monday, if they've managed to cheat their way all the way to voting day, DO NOT VOTE FOR THEM!

My mouth dropped open as I finished reading. I grabbed my cell phone and dialed Ivy. She answered on the first ring.

"Did you read it?" she asked.

"It's nuts!" I said. "It's a disaster!"

"You think?" Ivy asked. "According to this, I'm the one who supposedly went to her mother for help!"

"What are we going to do?" I asked.

I heard Ivy tapping her keyboard. Then she groaned.

"What?" I asked.

"The first time I read this, which was about an hour ago, there were eleven page views registered. Now there are fifty-one page views. Looks like the word is already spreading."

"Then we have to post something defending ourselves," I said.

"The four of us need to agree on what we're going to do," Ivy said. "We need to have an emergency meeting. School is letting out an hour early tomorrow for that dismissal drill. Can we meet at your house after school to deal with this?"

"My house?" I asked.

"Mine is too far away," Ivy said. "Plus, I'd really like to figure this out in a house my mother isn't lurking around in. If we know it can be at your house, the three of us can get permission notes from our parents, and we can take the bus with you."

"What are we going to do?" I asked. "If we lose the votes . . . how do we even get support back? Once you put something out there that somebody's cheating, everybody's going to keep wondering, right?"

"Paulie, one thing at a time," Ivy said. "Can we meet at your house?"

"Hang on," I said.

I ran down the stairs to my mother's study. She was at her desk, still wearing her sensible suit, but she'd replaced her shoes with slippers.

"Mom, can my CEP group meet here after school?" I asked.

She peered at me over her reading glasses. "You have early dismissal tomorrow," she said.

"I know—we'd just come here straight after."

My mother took a long pause, her expression dangerously "thoughtful." Sometimes she reacted to even a simple question as if she were being asked to consider refinancing the space program.

"I won't be home until five. But I think that would be okay. Honey, that casserole is still in the freezer. Did you and Kevin order pizza for dinner?"

She knew we'd ordered pizza because I'd left the box on the recycling pile.

"Sorry," I said. "He was starving, and I waited too long to defrost it. I've still got Ivy on the phone—I'm going to tell her it's okay."

When she didn't say no, I ran back upstairs.

"It's fine," I told Ivy.

"Okay, I'm going to text Tally and Miko right now," Ivy said.

"Who would do this?" I asked. "Somebody trying to win the funding themselves, probably, right? Did you notice how at one point it says 'we are not getting a pro to help us'—we—that means it was someone from one of the other groups, right?"

"We'll figure it out tomorrow," Ivy said. "I can't talk now—I don't want my mother to overhear something. I just hope she doesn't check the blog tonight."

"She's been checking the blog?" I asked.

"She pores over it like it's her job. She is endlessly fascinated with this whole thing, and if she gets wind of this, she'll make my life a nightmare. We'll figure everything out tomorrow, okay? I've gotta go."

She hung up without saying good-bye.

I tried to concentrate on my book report, but the bad feeling in my stomach continued to grow. I checked the blog again and gasped.

Eighty-four page views.

Stupid Internet! Was the whole school going to be talking about this tomorrow?

Like it or not, I would know the answer to that very soon.

· chapter ·

12

"Did you hear me? I'm timing you," Audriana said. "The point is to do the sit-ups at some point while you're being timed. Maybe even the whole time."

"Sorry," I said. I hadn't been able to think clearly since I'd first seen the blog last night. "I was just noticing how many girls happened to pick Pitch In T-shirts to wear to gym. How did they make so many shirts without going over budget, anyway?"

"They're not very flattering," Audriana said. "The huge T-shirt thing is so 1980s. Let me reset this stupid thing."

Audriana fiddled with the stopwatch.

"It can't be a coincidence," I said. "They planned this—it's all part of the whole crazy blog rumor. Why did we decide to have a blog in the first place? All it's done is give Pitch In a weapon to use against us."

"Look, if Ms. Zarin sees us just sitting here, she's

126

going to make us do laps. I cannot handle laps," Audriana said. "I ate cheese fries at lunch."

"Sorry," I said, lying back while Audriana fiddled with the stopwatch some more. "It's just that—"

Audriana grabbed my ankles. "Ready? Go," she commanded.

I started doing sit-ups as fast as I could. By the time I got to twenty, my stomach was starting to burn. Whoever invented the gym-class fitness tests was a mean, bitter, and probably out of shape middle-aged person. I struggled on, the space between sit-ups growing longer and longer.

"Stop," said Audriana. "Thirty-seven. My turn."

"Give me a minute." I groaned. "Ow. I just need a little breather."

I sat up and hugged my stomach. A tall girl in a Pitch In T-shirt was walking by. She shot me a mean look, narrowing her eyes and curling her lip into a sneer. Somehow I suspected the look was not because of my poor sit-up performance.

"Did you see that?" I asked Audriana.

"See what?"

"That girl, Kelly whatever. You know. She just shot this look of daggers at me. This has been happening to me all day."

"Oh, her. That's Sasha's BFF. I mean, that doesn't exactly surprise you, does it?"

"What do you mean?" I asked.

Audriana looked around for Ms. Zarin, who was impersonating a marine drill sergeant and loudly scolding an undersized eighth-grader over by the bleachers.

"Look, I'm Team *4 Girls* all the way, obviously," Audriana said. "I don't care if you guys cheated or not. But you can't expect the Pitch In people to feel the same way. You know how jocks are when things get competitive. Now, start timing me."

I stared at Audriana, my mouth hanging open, which must have looked especially gross since I was still out of breath.

"What do you mean you don't care if we cheated? You're really good friends with Tally—didn't she tell you the rumor is fake?"

"Tally has no idea what's going on," Audriana said. "I mean, when does she ever? Anyway, she's flipping out and avoiding you guys because she still hasn't finished her article."

Kelly walked by again, this time holding a clipboard. I caught her eye.

"Figuring out a way to cheat on your sit-ups, too?" Kelly asked, flouncing off before I could respond.

"This whole thing is insane," I said, shaking my head.

"Oh please, this is nothing," Audriana told me. "When we had auditions for *The Sound of Music* last fall, people were plotting, starting rumors, handing out cupcakes made by somebody whose brother had strep throat and supposedly licked the batter spoon—all kinds of stuff. Three girls who all wanted to play Maria practically murdered one another, and then Valerie Teale ended up getting the part. And we all know how that turned out. Boy, she was bad. She couldn't even learn all her lines! She wrote some of them on a piece of paper and taped it to the inside of her habit. Talk about cheating!"

"But we didn't—"

"Can you please start timing me before Ms. Zarin kicks us both out of class?" Audriana demanded.

She flopped down on her back and started doing sit-ups before I could get the stopwatch going. Ms. Zarin was now walking by, her eyes on me and Audriana. I stared at the stopwatch with fake concentration.

"Stop," I said when Ms. Zarin began wandering in the other direction.

"Great," Audriana wheezed. "How many did I do?"

The bell rang, and Ms. Zarin zoomed back toward us, collecting stopwatches. I made up a number.

"Uh, forty-seven," I said.

Great. Now I really was cheating.

Audriana looked surprised.

"Really? Wow. That's, like, a personal best for me.

And it's early dismissal—we're done for the day! See you later."

I stood up and headed for the door behind everyone else. Before I could go into the locker room, someone came out of the door and stopped right in front of me.

Sasha Hendricks.

"You," she said, pointing at me. "The magazine. You're one of the four, right? We need to talk."

"I've got to get to my bus," I said. But she stood right in my way.

"If you think I'm going to let you get away with cheating your way to the CEP money, you couldn't be more wrong," Sasha said, her face red with anger. "I play by the rules on the field and off, and if you're going up against me, you better do the same, or I will make it my business to take you down."

"I do play by the rules," I said.

Sasha made me nervous. It wasn't because she was so incredibly tall and powerfully built, though, that didn't help. She was just so . . . fierce. All "do it by the playbook" and stuff.

"Really? So this girl Ivy's mother doesn't work for some big-shot magazine?" Sasha asked.

"No," I said. "I mean yes, she used to. But she doesn't anymore."

"So are you denying it? This woman hasn't been approving all your work and giving you help?"

Actually, I didn't know the answer to that for sure. Ivy had said something about her mother going over everything. But even if that were true, did that make us cheaters? And what about the software—had Ivy's mother lent her something? And if she had, did that break the rules?

"This is all because of some stupid, anonymous post on a blog," I said. "If it were anything more than a rumor, why wouldn't the poster have identified themselves? Wouldn't you have put down your name if you wrote it?"

But we specifically said no real names on the blog, I thought. Although maybe Sasha didn't know that. Kelly and Alara came out of the locker room together, and they stopped when they saw me and Sasha. They came to stand on either side of her. *Great,* I thought. *Three against one.*

"Spreading accusations on a blog isn't my style," Sasha snapped, her hand on one hip. She towered over me. I felt like a bunny rabbit trying not to get stepped on by a horse. "It's cowardly, and I hate cowards as much as I hate cheaters. But wherever it came from, you better deal with it. You need to take this to Mrs. Finley, and you better do it soon. If you don't, I will."

Kelly looked angry, but Alara had a triumphant smile on her face.

Suddenly it hit me. *Alara posted that rumor,* I thought. I had no way to prove it, but something about the look on Alara's face made me certain I was right.

"I have to go," I said, pushing past them.

"I meant what I said," Sasha called after me. "You deal with it, or I will."

I made a beeline for the exit at the end of the hall and pushed the door open, relieved beyond belief to be outside in the chilly fall air.

Thankfully, no one from Pitch In came after me.

· chapter ·
13

Miko was already on the bus when I got there. She was sitting in the back with her iPod on, looking entirely unapproachable. Ivy had a spot near the front with her book bag on the empty seat next to her. She waved me over when she saw me.

"Boy, am I glad to see you," I said, sitting down beside her. My mind was still spinning from my encounter with Sasha. I felt like I had been about to realize something, and now I couldn't remember what. A hissing sound indicated the doors of the bus were closing. I heard a muffled pounding noise, and the doors opened again. Tally got on the bus, her coat buttoned wrong and her bag unzipped and dangerously close to losing its contents.

"I'm sooooo sorry," she exclaimed to the driver, handing over a note. "I got on the wrong bus. I think it was going to Canada!"

She collapsed in the front seat behind the driver and leaned forward, apparently to continue the story of her near miss accidentally leaving the country.

I looked at Ivy. "I can't take any more drama," I said. "I've gotten so much already today from people calling me a cheater, especially in gym."

"Me too," Ivy said. "Not that I care what people say to or about me. That's the least of my worries."

"You're lucky to be so thick-skinned," I said. "To be honest, Ivy, I'm really bad with confrontation. I've always tried to kind of fly under the radar—stay out of the way of the PQuits and the Alaras of the world and just do my thing. Before my friend Evelyn moved, I spent all my free time with her. We never went to dances or games or anything—I always told my mother I'd just rather hang with my friend. But the truth is, Ivy, I'm kind of spineless when it comes to people being mad at me. If it's going to get any worse than it was today . . ." I heaved an enormous sigh.

"I mean, I'm just not sure I can handle it," I continued. "If the whole school is going to be mad at me and calling me a cheater . . . I just, I'm not like you, Ivy. The whole thing ties my stomach in knots and makes me want to crawl into a hole and hide for the rest of the year."

Ivy rummaged in her bag for something and handed it to me. I thought she was going for a Kleenex, but it turned out to be a Twizzler. I didn't like licorice, but I took it, anyway, and held it in front of me uncertainly.

"However I look on the outside, I don't exactly enjoy confrontation, either," Ivy said. "And I'm really sorry about your friend. I know how that feels. But at the end of the day, you've got to realize you can't go through life trying to fly under the radar. You'll never really do anything that way. Playing it safe isn't always the best way to go. Anyway, you're not in this alone. Evelyn isn't here, but I am. And I'm your friend now. For whatever that's worth."

I nodded.

"You're right. And it's worth a lot," I added. "I'm really glad we're friends, and that's the truth." I gave Ivy a small smile.

"We'll get the rest sorted out," Ivy said. "Is your house far?"

I looked out the window. "No," I said. "It's the next stop, actually. I can walk it on a nice day."

"We'd better make sure Tally gets off the bus with us," Ivy said. "She might actually end up in Canada by mistake someday."

I stood up and looked toward the back of the bus. Miko was already putting her stuff away and heading up to meet us.

The house was quiet as I unlocked the front door and let everyone in.

"The living room is right in there," I said, pointing.

My mother always took people's coats when they visited.

"Um, anyone want to hang up their . . ."

Too late. This probably wasn't the best time to tell them we were a no-shoes house, either. I took mine off and left them by the door. When I walked into the living room, my group looked like they'd been hanging out for the better part of an hour waiting for me. Their coats were in a pile on the arm of the couch. Miko was sitting in the hard-back armchair with her legs crossed under her. Tally had plopped into the overstuffed and overused armchair and had sunk so deep into the cushion that from behind, it looked mostly like the chair had sprouted long, blond curls. Ivy was settling onto one side of the couch, her legs curled up next to her, shoes on the floor. She was wearing a long, warm-looking sweater jacket of mixed purples and greens, and her feet completed the picture. She had a green sock on her right foot and a purple sock on her left.

Ivy leaned forward to reach toward something on the coffee table. Something, I realized with dismay, that my mother had prepared and left there.

"And this would be what, exactly?" Ivy asked, holding up a quivering white cube skewered on the end of a toothpick.

I sighed. "Tofu, probably," I said. "My mother is on a major health food tear."

"Good to know," Ivy said, dropping the tofu back onto the plate. "Next time I'll bring my own snacks. We don't need the diversion, anyway. We apparently have quite a situation here."

"Yeah, what is going on?" Miko asked. "Nobody has said anything to my face, but I saw the thing on the blog, and I know people are up in arms, saying our group is cheating."

"I saw that, too," Tally said. "Y'all, this had nothing to do with me, I swear on my great-granny's Appalachian grave. I have no idea what this is all about."

"I think I might," I said.

Everyone looked at me. I sank down on the couch next to Ivy.

"What?" Ivy asked.

"Something happened before I got on the bus, and I think everything just clicked into place. Okay, you guys all know Alara Jameson, right?"

Everyone nodded. Tally opened her mouth to provide a more lengthy response, but I cut her off.

"Well, I think she might have been the one who posted the cheating thing. Alara has never liked me much. She goes out of her way to be nasty to me whenever she gets the chance. Which I guess is kind of my fault because I did something once that really upset her, but . . . story for another time. Anyway, I've managed to avoid her for the first week of school, until yesterday. I ran into her in the hall, and she started in with some rant about how lame our magazine was and how Pitch In was going to blow us out of the water, and that we were just amateurs way out of our league, and the whole school was laughing at us, stuff like that."

"And?" Miko asked.

"And I said a few things to her."

"What things?" Ivy asked, leaning slightly toward me.

"Just that she was wrong, I guess. That we really did know what we were doing, and we had a good chance at winning."

"That's it?" Miko said. "Then I'm missing something here."

"No," I said slowly.

The thing is, I was having trouble remembering exactly what it was I had said.

"Look, to be honest, she caught me off guard because I was walking down the hall talking to myself, and she heard me. I was embarrassed, and I guess I got defensive or something. Usually I'd just walk away, but for some reason I stood my ground and tried to tell her off. And I said something about Ivy's mother— about her being a magazine editor. I only meant that we weren't totally flying blind. Ivy would obviously know something about publishing because of her mom and, Ivy, you did say your mom kept going over what we were working on with you—"

"Your mother goes over everything we're doing?" Tally asked.

Ivy looked embarrassed, and I wanted to kick myself.

"I wouldn't put it that way, but yeah, she's on my case about it," Ivy told her. "She wants to see and hear every single detail. She's not telling me what to do. She's just interrogating me to death about it. Do no one else's parents do that?"

"Mine do," Miko said, scowling and playing with a suede tassel that hung from the top of her boot.

"My mom does, too," I said. "I didn't mean it in a bad way. It was just something I blurted out to Alara because she said we had no idea what we were doing."

"Okay, but what about the part of the post that says Ivy's mother is having her company do our layout?" Miko said. "Because, are you kidding me? I've been making myself crazy figuring out the design program she recommended. It took me two days just to get the stupid thing downloaded and working on my computer. If *City Nation* magazine is laboring night and day to do my job for me, I'd sure like to know about it."

"They're not," Ivy said sharply.

"And I didn't tell Alara they were," I added quickly. "I mean, yeah, Ivy got the name of that program from her mother," I said, "but I didn't even go into that. I just said our design was going to be really polished or something like that."

"Wait—so I'm going to get in trouble for taking a software suggestion from a professional?" Miko said, her voice rising.

"Nobody is in trouble," I exclaimed. "That was all I said about the magazine. Alara twisted my words."

"And Alara hates you so much she decided to get back at you by putting a story on the blog? Why?" Tally asked.

I sighed. I was pretty sure I knew the answer to that, too.

"The original thing she was mad about was a long time ago, but I basically laughed at her for saying something stupid in a class. Then yesterday, I said something along the lines of *4 Girls* being more important than Pitch In, which she basically took as me saying that she was stupid and I was a better person because I get good grades or whatever. I guess it must be a supersensitive topic for her or something."

"Yeah, it sounds like you might have really hit her where it hurts," Ivy said. "So she hit back on the blog."

"So we think we know who did it and why," Tally said. "Can't we just forget about it now?"

"The whole school has probably read it," Ivy said. "We can't assume it's just going to go away. We've got a bad rap now. We're supposed to be providing a voice for girls and giving them a place to express their own. How can we do that if they don't trust us?"

"And Sasha Hendricks said she was going to go to the principal about it," I added.

Miko's mouth dropped open in dismay, and Tally slapped her hands over her face.

"When were you going to tell us *that*?" Ivy asked.

"Right now," I said. "This all just happened right before I got on the bus."

"I cannot believe this," Miko said loudly. "This is serious. We really could be disqualified!"

I looked at Ivy, who was shaking her head.

"Yeah, this makes it worse than I thought," Ivy said. "What a mess."

"We're going to get kicked out?" Tally asked. "This is like that episode of *Law & Order* where—"

"Tally, this isn't a *television* show," Miko barked.

Tally looked taken aback by Miko's words. She opened her mouth to say something, then bit her lip.

"Tally, it's okay, everyone's just emotional right now," Ivy said.

Miko rolled her eyes.

"It's just . . . ," Ivy continued. "I mean, I for one have a lot riding on this project. I'm not doing it just for fun."

"Oh, but the rest of us are?" Miko shot back.

Ivy's face went red with anger. "What is it with you, Miko? It's like there's nothing I can say that doesn't enrage you. I didn't say you were doing the project for fun. I don't know anything about you. All I know is how you've acted and what I've heard you say, which is that this project is a huge inconvenience for you forced on you by your parents, not to mention a personal embarrassment of the highest order, since you can barely stand to speak to me if one of your friends is around."

Miko stood up. "You're right about one thing, Ivy—you don't know anything about me," she snapped. "So let me enlighten you. I have a lot riding on this project, too. You have no idea how much pressure I have on me. I take three accelerated classes and have parents who don't settle for anything less than an A. And yes, since you're so interested all of a sudden, my parents did tell me I had to enter the CEP competition. But I came up with the magazine idea by myself because I figured I might as well do something I found interesting and might be good at. But my parents still aren't happy because they think I picked something too easy for my project.

"And do my friends give me a hard time because of the magazine? Yeah, they kind of do. Are they judgmental and exclusive and even mean sometimes? Yep. Do they think slogging for good grades and extra credit is lame? Absolutely. Do they like you personally, Ivy? No. Mostly because Shelby told them not to, and you know the reason why. Shelby might rub you the wrong way, but she was completely humiliated when you blew her off in front of both your mothers that night you all met. If you don't like her, that's your business, but she's my best friend. So I'm sorry if she doesn't meet with your approval, and I'm sorry we can't all be as supercool as you with your Manhattan hair and your vintage clothes. It doesn't even matter—the only thing you need to know is, no. You are not the only one with a lot riding on this. And if we get disqualified from this competition, you are not the one who's going to have to face my parents and tell them that—"

Miko's voice broke off suddenly, and she burst into tears.

I was stunned. I'd been at the same school with Miko since kindergarten, and I could never, not once, remember seeing her cry.

Ivy looked completely taken aback. "I'm sorry if—I didn't mean to imply that . . . ," she began.

Miko dropped back down, wiping her face with her

sleeve. "Forget it," she said, her voice steady again.

"No," Ivy said. "Listen. I was starting to say I didn't mean to imply that this wasn't a big deal for you, but maybe I really was implying that."

I stared at Ivy—what was she doing?

"What I'm trying to say is, I probably sounded like I was judging you," Ivy continued. "You're right, I don't know you, Miko. I made up my mind about you the minute I realized you hung out with Shelby, and I didn't give you a chance after that, even though you've worked just as hard on this project as I have. Maybe harder. So I am sorry."

Miko looked up and met Ivy's eye. The two stared at each other for a moment, then Miko nodded.

"It's okay," Miko said. She glanced at Tally, then looked over at me. "I'm sorry to get all upset. I'm just really worried that this is going to become some kind of official school problem."

"This is all my fault," I said. "I am so sorry."

"Don't, Paulina. It's Alara's fault," Miko said.

"Whoever's fault it is, it's out there now. So what are we going to do about it?" Ivy said. "Alara seems like she's all talk, but if Sasha Hendricks says she's going to the principal, I bet she'll follow through on it."

"She said she would if we didn't first," I corrected.

"Like we're going to rat ourselves out?" Miko said. "I don't think so."

"I think that's exactly what we should do," Ivy said.

"Why?" Tally asked.

"We've been accused publicly of cheating," Ivy said. "On our own blog, to add insult to injury. We know pretty much everyone has heard or will hear something about it. And we know the chances are good that it's going to be brought to Principal Finley's attention. So I say we send the principal an e-mail today—right now. We explain what happened, what the facts are. We let her know that we want to make sure she doesn't have any problem with our group and that we haven't violated any rules—that we haven't cheated. If she agrees, we post her response on the website, and full steam ahead."

"And if she disagrees?" I asked. "If she thinks that our getting the software information from your mom or her checking in on our progress is some kind of issue?"

Ivy shrugged. "If she thinks it's a problem, then we're out," she said. "Because those things really happened. At least this way, we've been up front about it. We heard there was a question. We passed the information along to the principal. What more can we do?"

"We could just keep our mouths shut," Tally suggested quietly.

"No, Ivy's right," Miko said. "We should put

together an e-mail from the four of us. Hopefully Principal Finley will get back to us by Monday, and then either way we'll know for sure. We won't have this hanging over us anymore."

"Let's do it then. I'll get my laptop," I said.

Minutes later, all four of us were squished onto the couch.

"Okay, so how about: A blog entry containing an accusation of cheating has recently come to our attention, in which we are accused of taking professional help and advice from a professional—wait, that's using the word twice in one sentence," Ivy said.

"Leave the beginning of that sentence, then just provide the link to the blog," Miko suggested. "Let her read it for herself so we're not trying to restate anything."

"Good idea," I said, pulling the blog link from my browser history and pasting it into the text. "Then we can say something like this: While Ivy Scanlon's mother has been following our progress closely, she has not contributed any advice, suggestions, or guidance to Ivy or to anyone else working on the magazine."

"Yeah, that's good," Ivy said. "And accurate. Just add 'other than providing the website address for a downloadable design program available to anyone free of charge.' We want to make sure we're including everything Alara hit us with."

"Okay," I said, typing. "And then something like 'while we do not believe we are in any violation of the CEP rules, we wanted to bring this to your attention, and ask that you provide us with an official response.'"

"That sounds good," Miko said.

"And we could add 'we humbly throw ourselves at the mercy of your office,'" Tally added helpfully.

"That's a thought," I said, not typing it in. "Okay. Everybody read it through, and then I'll put our names on it."

I sat back and waited as they read.

"Looks good to me," Ivy said.

"I agree," Miko added.

"Where's the part about throwing ourselves at the mercy of her office?" Tally asked.

"I'm not sure," I told her. "But do you think this looks okay?"

"It's very professional," Tally decided.

"Okay, then," I said. I tapped out a few more strokes on the keyboard.

Respectfully yours,
Ivy Scanlon
Miko Suzuki
Tally Janeway
Paulina Barbosa

It was the first time we'd ever seen our names together. In print. It was strange. And kind of cool.

"Should I hit Send?" I asked. "We can't take it back once she gets it."

Tally reached around me and hit Send.

"Done," she said. "So now we wait, right?"

"Right," Ivy said.

"So I guess there's no point in putting in any work on the project right now, I mean not until we know for sure whether we're still in . . ."

Tally's voice trailed off as we all stared at her.

"Um, except that I've got this perfectly and completely finished article just clogging up my hard drive, which I will definitely send out to y'all the second I get home, or at least before midnight," Tally said. "Almost finished, I mean."

"That's what I thought you were going to say," I declared.

"But before I go, I have to eat something before I perish of hunger," Tally announced.

She grabbed one of the tofu cubes and popped it in her mouth. Then her eyes grew wide, and she daintily spit the cube onto her palm, pulled a napkin from the pile, and folded it up like a little gift.

"Y'all, what exactly is tofu?" she asked.

"Oh, you know," I said. "Monkey brain, mostly, isn't that right, guys?"

"In a gelatin base," added Ivy.

"Usually thickened with a little essence of fish liver," Miko added.

Tally screwed up her face and waved her hands at the plate of tofu, like she was trying to use ESP waves to send it away.

"But monkeys are practically human! Eating their brains is like canon-bulling!"

"Well, yeah, that's the best part," Miko said.

Tally gave a little shriek, then she saw me trying not to laugh. I failed when I heard Miko start to giggle and Ivy chime in with an all-out cackle.

When Tally started to laugh, too, that set me off all over again.

It was the first time the four of us had ever laughed together at the same time.

I must have checked my e-mail hundreds of times that weekend. I only took a break on Saturday afternoon, when Ivy and I met for cappuccinos, where we promised not to discuss anything magazine related. We stuck to the subjects of boys, bagels, and the best conditioner for winter hair. By Sunday night I'd had seventeen back and forth e-mails with Evelyn (and one video chat), but no word from Principal Finley. The only thing that came in that had anything to do with the magazine was Tally's long overdue article, which finally appeared in my in-box just as I was getting ready to go to bed.

When we were little, it seems like most girls thought it was cool to get good grades. Now that I'm in seventh grade, I'm getting the feeling more and more of us act like it's cool

not to, and I guess I'm no exception. I pretend I don't care that school can be really hard for me. I don't talk about this thing my brain does that makes it hard for me to concentrate or remember what I'm supposed to remember. I go along with it when people act like the important thing now is maybe how you look, who you hang out with, and how they look and who they hang out with . . . but I can't help wondering. If you don't do well in school right now, is that it forever? If you're not in the smart crowd, does that mean you'll never be smart? It's like we've hit the year where we're supposed to choose who we are.

Maybe some people reading this saw our drama club adaptation of *Anne of Green Gables* last spring, starring yours truly as Anne. Anyway, there's a scene in it where Anne's friend Diana asks her if she thinks it's better to be smart or pretty. And I always wondered . . . better for WHO? Do we even have a say in those things?

Seventh grade is starting to feel like the time we all agree what part we're going to play. Whether we're going to be smart or pretty. Into sports or computers. Among a bunch of other stuff. And when that gets figured out, when I know if my character is a loudmouth or a superrich kid or a scholarship nerd, it feels like

I'll be stuck with that character forever. Or at least until graduation.

I guess what I'm saying is, why do we have to pick our personalities now? Do we have to pick them at all? Can't we be maybe part brain and part princess with mad computer skills? How about half drama queen, half jock who is also a bookworm? Maybe we could all just give one another a little slack in that area. 'Cause I loved being in *Anne of Green Gables*. But if that was the only part I was ever going to play, and I had to be in it every single day and be that exact same person and never change, I think I'd go nuts. I want to do more plays and get a bunch of parts and be all different kinds of people.

Don't you?

I got what Tally was trying to say. I was sitting on my bed trying to fix some of her sentence fragments while still keeping her voice, and I must have fallen asleep. I didn't wake up until the next morning when my cell phone began to ring. I was so tired I didn't recognize the sound and kept hitting the Snooze button on my alarm. After a minute my exhausted brain realized I should be reaching for a different beeping device. Somehow I found my phone and pressed it to my ear.

"Hello?"

"Did you check your e-mail?"

"Ivy?" I asked. I was in that was-just-in-a-deep-sleep haze. Was I supposed to be somewhere?

"We're in the clear!"

I sat up.

"What?"

"Principal Finley sent out an e-mail at six AM. Does she always start work that early do you think? Anyway, read it yourself, but the gist of it is we're in the clear. She's got no problem with us. We've done nothing wrong. We're fine!"

"We're fine?"

There was a pause.

"I woke you, didn't I?" Ivy said. "I have to get up with the birds around here. The bus comes at the crack of dawn. Yes, Paulie. We are fine!"

"We're fine," I repeated.

"Girl, get yourself a shower and a hot cup of coffee. I'll see you at school, okay?"

"Okay," I said.

I snapped my phone shut and sat on the edge of my bed, a smile breaking over my face as Ivy's words sunk in. There was a thud outside my door, then a knock. Kevin burst in without waiting for me to answer.

"There's a *huge* spider in the bathroom! You've got to come see it. It's awesome!"

He dashed out, leaving the door open.

I got up and grabbed my robe and a plastic cup suitable for spider capture and release. From down the hall, I heard my mother shriek.

"Don't hurt it," Kevin yelled. "I'm keeping him!"

We were fine. I felt absolutely fabulous, and no spider was going to mess with that.

• • • • • • •

"So I hear you guys are back in the game."

I closed my locker and turned around.

It was too early in the morning for me to see Benny Novak. Actually, at the moment it felt like it was too early in my *life* to see Benny Novak.

"Um, yeah?" I half said, half asked.

Why do boys always look so adorable when they are rumpled-looking and their hair is messed up and their eyes still sleepy? Or was it just *this* boy?

"No, I just mean word got around this morning. You know. After I saw that thing on your blog, I wondered how it would turn out."

"You read our blog?"

Oops! It came out sounding like an accusation, and Benny must have heard it that way because his face turned red.

"No, of course not!" he said. "I mean, obviously I don't go around reading girl blogs. But people were talking about it, so I heard. Anyway. Forget it."

He started to go, and I called after him. "No, sorry. I knew what you meant. The whole school was talking about it, so obviously pretty much everyone heard . . ."

My words trailed off when he turned to face me. I remembered that his eyes were this deep ocean-blue. I remembered every single reason why his existence had turned me into a tower of Jell-O last spring. Just smile at him, my inner Voice of Evelyn commanded. My lips ignored it.

"But yeah, we got the okay from the spider's office," I said.

Oh. No.

"The principal's office, I mean," I corrected quickly. "Sorry, there was also this spider in my bathroom when the e-mail . . . I mean, no. Yeah."

I wasn't fit to be anyone's editor or to be allowed anywhere near the English language at this moment.

"So she e-mailed the official announcement this morning."

"Right," Benny said. "I saw it. Heard about it, or . . . heard something. So, good. Congratulations."

"Thanks," I said.

There was a sudden explosion of loud male voices. Benny glanced toward them. I registered only a blur of varsity jackets and many legs.

"Anyway, catch you later," he said.

"Right, you too," I replied.

He was already gone, so I made a face. "Must. Speak. English," I told myself out loud.

"Hey! Who are you talking to? Did you see Benny Novak just now? Is he like a baby Taylor Lautner or what? What class do you have first period? Are you going to social studies today? Can you believe it?"

To myself I answered all the questions: I saw him, yes, bio, yes, yes.

"Yes," I told Tally. It seemed to work for most of her questions. "Ivy called me as soon as the e-mail came in," I added as we walked toward the classroom.

"What e-mail?" Tally asked.

I gave her a look.

"Can I believe what?" I asked.

"That Ms. Zoundfrown broke her foot. We're going to have a sub today, and who knows, maybe for longer! What e-mail?"

It must be nice to be Tally sometimes, I thought. She was probably the only one who hadn't spent the weekend stressing over our situation.

"From Principal Finley," I said. "About our little problem? The response to the e-mail we all wrote on Friday. You didn't see it?"

Tally came to a dead stop. She put her hand on my arm.

"Oh my gosh. Okay. Just tell me, Paulina. I can take it."

I was tempted to draw it out, but I couldn't.

"We're fine," I told her. "Mrs. Finley said there's absolutely no problem."

"No way!"

"Way," I assured her.

Tally reached out and grabbed me in a killer hug, smothering me in curls and the smell of shampoo.

"Good thing I wrote my article then," she said.

I shook my head.

"Tally, you are nuts," I told her. "I've got to go upstairs. I have a double bio period today. What do you have first period? Where's your book bag?"

Tally froze, then snapped her head around to see that her bag really wasn't there.

"I have no idea!" she exclaimed.

"You'd better retrace your steps," I told her. "Where were you last?"

Tally's face went blank. "I don't remember," she said.

"It isn't even first period. Bus, locker, library maybe?"

Tally gave a gasp and rushed away.

I smiled and walked up the stairs to the bio classroom. Our teacher, Mr. Pilsen, was usually late, and today was no exception. This was the one class I had with Miko because our class and the accelerated session were combined for lab double periods. Everyone seemed fairly rowdy for a Monday morning, and several guys were taking advantage of Mr. Pilsen's lateness to toss a football around. Miko was sitting at her desk and flipping through her textbook and ignoring the activity going on around her. She looked up when I walked into the room, smiled, and gestured for me to come over. I had to work to not have a surprised look on my face or turn around to see if she was actually waving to someone standing behind me.

"So you saw it, right?" I asked.

Miko nodded. "I cannot even tell you how relieved I am," she said. "I was so stressed this weekend I could barely sleep. I was so scared we were going to be disqualified."

"Me too!" I said, sitting at the empty desk next to her. "I checked my e-mails obsessively."

"I couldn't check mine at all," Miko said. "I seriously felt like throwing up every time I thought about it. I figured if there was news over the weekend, you'd call me to let me know."

"Oh, definitely," I said. Though I wasn't sure I would have done that in reality. Calling Miko's house—or her cell phone . . . it would seem so weird. Or would it anymore?

"So listen, though," Miko said. "We're back in the running, but we're way behind schedule now."

"How far behind?" I asked.

"Well, like I said, I was really stressed about the whole thing. So I didn't exactly do a lot of work on it this weekend. I mean, the really big stuff is done already. I figured out the program and finished the framework of the cover design and the layout for all the articles except Tally's, which I only just got. But I can't actually do anymore until we come up with a cover article, and that kind of got dropped over the weekend, at least by me."

I groaned. The cover article was the one thing I'd totally forgotten about. We'd all lost sight of it because of the blogpost.

"You're right," I said. "And Ivy says the latest she can bring the finished file to the printer is by the end of business hours on Wednesday. That's the day after tomorrow! We need a chunk of time to work on this together."

"That's what I was thinking," Miko said. "But honestly, I don't know when. I've got a study session for the math state exam after school today, and those are nonnegotiable in my house. Plus, I have a book report due tomorrow, which I have to finish tonight."

"I have the book report due, too," I said. "I think we all do."

"And I've got a violin lesson right after school tomorrow," Miko continued. "Which there's no way my mother would ever let me skip—not even if those aliens finally got here and started blasting away at us with space rays."

Had everyone heard about these aliens?

"That leaves tomorrow evening," I said.

"Which is cutting it awfully close," Miko added. "Plus, this could be hours of work. How are we going to swing it, unless we stay up half the night, which we can't do together?"

I opened my mouth, then closed it. Then opened it again.

"Wait, though. What if you all came to my house and brought sleeping bags and stuff for the morning," I said. "We could have a work party."

"A sleepover?" Miko asked. "On a school night?"

"I know, but it's not, like, a just-for-fun thing. If I explain to my mother it is seriously for school, and there is absolutely no other way, she might be okay with it."

Miko knit her eyebrows together and chewed on her lower lip.

"You're thinking your parents will say no?" I asked.

She nodded.

"Well, what if you tell them that if you can't do the sleepover, we're going to miss our deadline and be out of the running for the CEP? That skipping the sleepover is an automatic *lose* for our group. Which is the truth. I mean, no offense, but it sounds like your parents are all about the win. Or maybe I'm wrong?"

Miko looked at me. "No, that's what it is," she said.

"They are definitely all about the win. Yeah, you know, if I put it to them that way, they might go for it. I mean, if it were Shelby or Daphne's house I was going to, they'd forbid it. But they know I'd never—"

Miko cut herself off.

"Never be caught dead at a sleepover just for fun at my house?" I asked with a grin.

I just knew Miko too well now to be worried about whether she liked me. I realized that she did like me, at least a little. I also knew it was still uncool for her to be hanging out with me or at my house. It was so much easier to just treat it like a joke. Maybe Ivy was starting to rub off on me because I really was beginning to care less about stuff like this.

"Okay, that might work in our favor, too," Miko said with a little smile. "Anyway, let me check. We should probably text Tal and Ivy right now, too, and get them to ask their parents."

"Sheesh, and I better call my mother and clear this with her," I said. "I'll be right back. If Mr. Pilsen shows up, I'm in the bathroom, okay?"

We weren't supposed to call people on our cell phones during school hours, but people usually got away with it in the girls' room.

Miko nodded. "Okay. Monday morning, though, he's usually fifteen minutes late, bare minimum, so you probably have time."

I ran to the girls' room, where I called my mother and got her to agree to host three overnight, frantically working guests. I have to hand it to my mom, though she often questions me relentlessly, she usually clues in pretty quickly when there are special circumstances. I sent quick texts to Ivy and Tally, then hightailed it back to bio. I got through the door just as Mr. Pilsen was arriving.

"Thumbs-up," I whispered to Miko. "And I texted the other girls."

"Good," she said. "I'm going to have to wait until after school. This is going to be hard enough—my mother isn't going to have a discussion like this with me on the phone."

"Okay," I told her.

"People," Mr. Pilsen was saying. "I'd like to talk about the skeletal structure and muscle makeup of the human body."

That makes one of us, I thought. My mind was spinning. I'd thought all weekend we might be disqualified, learned just hours ago that we were back in the running, and was now worried we weren't going to make our deadline. But I opened my notebook and tried to get rid of all thoughts that weren't skeleton and muscle related.

Peeking over at Miko, I watched her take detailed notes in tiny, perfect handwriting. She looked as put together as ever. To most people, she'd look like she did every day—a PQuit with no problems except the double science period preventing her from hanging out with her fabulous friends.

But now I knew that things weren't always the way they appeared to be on the surface. It was like Mr. Pilsen was saying—beneath our exterior are all these complicated layers of muscle and nerve and bone. Who would ever know by just looking at us from the outside?

You just had to see some things to believe them.

· chapter ·

15

My room looked like a glimpse into a parallel universe—familiar, but different. The weird factor was provided by the presence of Ivy Scanlon, Tally Janeway, and Miko Suzuki, all in their pajamas.

Three laptops were open and powered up, placed around the room on the floor. In one corner was a heap of sleeping bags, pillows, and overnight cases. By the door was the shopping bag Ivy had brought, overflowing with Twizzlers, boxes of cakey things, and an enormous Ziploc bag filled with something that looked like Cap'n Crunch. The house still smelled like the pizzas we'd tucked into for dinner.

"I'm so full I'm going to pass out," Tally declared. She had flopped onto my bed in her purple flannel pajama bottoms and an oversized T-shirt bearing a faded likeness of the original Broadway cast of *Wicked*.

"No passing out," Ivy commanded. "It's already

eight, and we have way too much to do."

"That's right," Miko agreed. "Get up and make your blood circulate. Do some yoga poses or something."

Tally groaned, but she sat up obediently, opening her eyes unnaturally wide.

"So what now?" I asked Ivy.

"The cover topic," she said. "Miko can't do anymore until it's done."

"What are we doing the cover story on again?" asked Tally.

I sighed. "We haven't even finished narrowing it down, remember, Tal?" I said. "This is what that long, wordy conversation was while we were eating. Ring a bell?"

"Oh, don't say eating," Tally said, falling back on the bed.

"There's one other thing I've been thinking about," Miko said. "An idea."

"Thank goodness," I said. "Don't keep us in suspense."

Miko took a deep breath and leaned over to grab the handle of Ivy's shopping bag. "Hey, I love Twizzlers. Can I have one of these?"

"My Twizzlers are your Twizzlers," Ivy said.

"Thanks. Okay," Miko said, ripping open the bag. "So when we all signed up to do this CEP thing over the summer, obviously none of us had any idea what we were getting ourselves into."

"That's the truth as I know it," Tally said, still on her back.

"And I don't mean the extra work. I expected that part. I just thought I'd be doing it by myself. I'm talking about the four of us getting thrown together. I mean, we're not exactly the same or anything."

"I know, right?" Ivy agreed. She was wearing silk pajamas in a deep purple and frankly looked amazing.

"So here's the thing," Miko continued. "We're figuring out how to work together because we basically had no choice, and on top of that we get blindsided with this cheating thing. From the beginning it just felt, to me, anyway, like it went from being me versus you to us four against half the school. Which, if you actually think about it, is kind of, like, the point. You know, dealing with the fact that we're different people with different lives, but trying to find a common voice as girls in all that. So I've been wondering—what if we make our topic the story of Pitch In?"

Huh? I'd been right there with Miko until the last sentence.

"You mean about them going up against us and the cheating thing? I'm not sure I see it. I mean, what's the point?" I asked.

"No, I actually mean the opposite," Miko responded.

She took a bite of a Twizzler and chewed it, looking thoughtful. "It's like, we could use *4 Girls* to focus on their need for funding for the softball team. Theoretically we could write about all three of the other groups, but we don't have that kind of time, and from everything I've heard, the sponsor-a-child thing fizzled out, and the book club isn't doing much better. But Pitch In is going really strong, and if we want an issue that affects all girls in school in some way, it seems like that might be it."

"So you're basically saying we should use our group to promote theirs?" Ivy asked.

Miko folded the rest of her Twizzler into a U-shape.

"It's probably stupid," Miko said.

"It's not stupid," Ivy said. "It's brilliant."

Miko straightened the Twizzler, listening.

"I think I agree," I said. "What better way to show girls that we can all pull together than by us showing support for our main rivals? But we've only got a few hours—can we get enough information on them to write something decent?"

"They've got that website," Tally said.

"That's right," Ivy said. "They've got a mission statement, bios of all the girls on the team, and they even have a link to some video interviews and some footage of the team in practice."

"Everybody pull up the page," I said.

Miko was one step ahead and already had the site opened on her laptop.

"I'm there," she said. "Just e-mailed you the link."

Tally was the only one who hadn't brought a laptop. She reluctantly hauled herself off my bed and took a spot on the floor next to me so she could look over my shoulder.

"Oh, let's include this reference to the law change," Ivy said. "Somebody google it—it's Title Fourteen, or Twelve, some number. Congress passed it in the 1970s, I know that."

Miko started typing.

"Title Nine," she said. "Equal opportunities in school for every student regardless of race, gender, or creed—and it says it made a huge difference in school athletic programs for girls."

"Perfect, yeah," Ivy said. "Bookmark that page, okay?"

"Is there a way to look up our boys' lacrosse team?" I asked. "I know they're new, but I can't remember what year they actually started."

"Oh, there was a big article on that in the local paper," Tally said. "With pictures. I remember there was a huge uproar at school because that senior, John van Something, got cropped out of the picture, and this other guy's mother was the photo editor at the paper, and the two guys got into this huge screaming match about it in the cafeteria, which I distinctly remember was a Wednesday, because it was taco day, and I looooove their tacos even though once I was eating one and I found a—"

"Whoa, overshare," Miko said, making the international "stop" gesture with her hand. "We should be able to find that article online. Yep, I've got a link to it. Okay, the boys' lacrosse team started up last year, same as the girls' softball team."

"And they got all new equipment before the season was even over," I said. "New uniforms, new pads, new sticks, even new helmets with the team name on them and this logo somebody came up with of an eagle and a mountain."

Ivy arched an eyebrow at me.

"Benny Novak is a lacrosse player," I mumbled. "So I may have subconsciously noticed a few details."

Miko glanced at me. "He's totally into you, by the way."

"Wuh?" I tried to reply.

"Benny Novak. He's started hanging around your locker in the mornings, and he stares at you during lunch when he thinks no one's looking," Miko said, her eyes still on her computer screen.

Yes!!! But . . . during . . . lunch? When sprouts and dressing hang out of my mouth? No!!!

"Miko, stop," Ivy said. "Paulina's going to flip out,

and nobody is allowed to do that until we're done working."

Miko smiled. "Okay," she said.

My lips moved, but no sound came out.

"Paulie, seriously. Snap out of it for a moment," Ivy said. "Do you still have the copy of the original Pitch In flyer?"

I blinked a few times. "Oh. You know, I actually do," I said, successfully distracted. "It's right here in my notebook."

"Okay, great. We can use a little material from that, too," Ivy said. "And then there are these team bios. Let's pick a few people, Sasha obviously and one or two others, and say who they are, put in some of these stats about the other teams they're on—the bit about the volleyball team going to regionals, things like that."

"We can include them as little sidebars of text. And I can take a screen grab from this video of the team," Miko said. "So we'll have a photo of them together."

"Oh, y'all, this is great," Tally said. "I get so tired of girl versus girl, you know? We're all in this together, after all."

"Hey, that's a good sentence," I said, opening a new document and typing it. "Let's use it."

"Yeah? I came up with a sentence that's good?" Tally asked.

"Yep—it's got a subject, a verb, an object, and everything," I told her.

"No way!"

"Way," Ivy said. "Tally, can you go through the bios and list a couple of the facts we were talking about?"

"Oh, okay, you mean like name and age and what other teams they've been on? Like volleyball?"

We all looked at Tally simultaneously.

"What?" she asked.

"Nothing," I said. "It's just, you didn't have to ask what we were talking about. You even remembered details."

"Well, don't get all used to it or anything," Tally said good-naturedly, taking my notebook and pen out of my hands. "Click the bios page, Paulina, so I can start."

We played musical laptops for the next hour, trading off taking notes, pulling up different sites, writing down information, and offering each other suggestions.

"That might be enough to start with," Miko finally said. "I've only budgeted a page and a half for the text, plus the picture and the sidebars with a few bios."

"Paulie, can you take a crack at stringing these notes together to draft something?" Ivy asked.

"Yep," I said.

"I've got the template for the layout on my screen," Miko said. "I just copied the cover art in from my flash drive. We need to settle on a font for the interior text, though."

Ivy slid over next to Miko and leaned in close to her.

"Which ones do you think look best?" Ivy asked.

Miko said something technical I didn't understand, but Ivy seemed to.

I turned my attention back to typing the draft, and my sense of time warped. I think I even forgot the other three were there a few times because I know I was muttering to myself.

I snapped back to reality when Miko made a loud sound of frustration. I didn't know how much time had gone by, but I'd finished the last paragraph. The article was almost done.

"Why is it doing that?" Miko exclaimed. "I copied in the whole text from Word, but it won't let me add paragraph spaces now."

"How about you all take a break from that and read this," I said, standing up and stretching my legs. "My feet are falling asleep. I have to move around."

I pushed the laptop toward them with my foot, then took a few unsteady steps.

"Oh. I fixed it," Miko said.

"Can we make changes as we read?" Ivy asked.

"Go right ahead," I said.

"Well, in this part, mentioning the year the Title Nine law was signed seems like it comes out of the blue. We could move the whole thing down and make that a separate paragraph," Miko said.

"Yeah, much better," Ivy agreed.

I was relieved to leave it to them for a few moments. My eye fell on Ivy's shopping bag of snacks. A box of Ring Dings caught my attention. I stared at it longingly.

"Ring Dings," I whispered.

"Paulie, have some," Ivy said.

I didn't need to be told twice.

"Oooh, I want one," Tally said.

I opened the box and tossed her a pack.

"And that needs to be changed to the plural," Miko was saying to Ivy.

"Got it," Ivy said. "E-mailed it to you. Can we just try this text in the template and see how the length is looking?"

Miko tapped a few buttons. "Okay. How's this?" she asked.

"Now it's there, but the font is tiny," Ivy said.

Miko hit a few more buttons and groaned.

"What?" I asked.

"Now the text is normal size, but the type has gone from black to green," she said.

I took a massive bite of Ring Ding. I can only say that while I probably looked ridiculous, the taste was epically worth it.

"Okay," Miko said. "It's the right color again. Hey, this is beginning to come together."

Tally knelt behind Ivy and Miko, a half-eaten Ring Ding in one hand.

"It looks like a real magazine!" Tally exclaimed.

"It *is* a real magazine," Ivy said. "Seriously, though, Miko, this looks great."

"Yeah? What about the cover?" Miko asked.

"Oh, can I see it?" I asked.

"It's right here," Miko said. "I'll enlarge it to full screen."

I crouched down next to them.

"Oh, boy," I said, taking it all in.

Miko had created cover art with a deep-purple sky as the background, lit by an enormous glowing moon dotted with stars. On every star was a girl—some riding them, some swinging, some hanging underneath. The girls ranged from tiny to large—some were blond, some dark, some with wild, curly hair, and another with a short pixie cut. They wore school uniforms, team outfits, ballet clothes, swimsuits, and pajamas. They held books or microphones or balls or rubber duckies or calculators. The top of the sky had no stars, and instead was the title in vivid, eye-popping green.

➍GIRLS

PITCHING IN FOR PITCH IN

VOLUME 1_ISSUE 1

"We can come up with a different title," Miko said. "I just took that from the article."

"It's perfect," I said. "The whole thing is perfect."

"The cover is outstanding," Ivy said. "You did an incredible job, Miko."

"Did you draw that?" Tally asked, looking amazed.

"Yeah. I used a program called ArtRage," Miko said. "I sketched the outline onto a digital tablet and did the rest on-screen."

"That is so good," Tally said. "I could never make something like that. Did you know I was the first kid at my preschool to ever fail finger painting? They actually made me take remedial finger painting lessons. They had to fly in a specialist from Sweden. Can you believe that?"

"I actually *can* believe it," I said, giving Tally an impulsive hug. "You are so unique."

"Oh, I am," Tally agreed.

"While we're all squished here, you two look at the text for the cover article," Miko said. "Ivy and I made a few fixes, and I added a screen grab of the team picture from their video, but we can still change the text. I haven't saved it into final."

I read the article, which looked totally different in its nice magazine font, all neatly laid out in block paragraphs.

"This should be two sentences," I said, pointing.

"Just change it," Miko said. I reached over her and

did it. I kept reading, making a few more little fixes as I went.

There was a knock on the door, and my mother peered cautiously into the room. She took in the sight of us hunched around the laptop and glanced at the Ring Ding wrappers and soda bottles littering the room. I stood up and gave her a look-how-dutifully-I'm-laboring-and-ignore-all-the-junk-food smile.

"Well. It certainly looks as if you all are working hard," she said.

It must have taken a huge effort for my mother to resist commenting on the importance of wholesome, organic foods in fueling brain activity. I give credit where credit is definitely due.

"We are. I think we're in the home stretch," I said.

"Well, more power to you. I for one can't wait to see the finished product," my mother said. "Let me know if you need anything."

With one final, concerned glance at the now-empty Ring Ding box, my mother gave us all a bright smile and backed gracefully out of the room.

"She's nice," Miko said. "It's very cool of her to let us do this."

"Thanks," I replied. "I guess it sort of is."

Historians may wish to take note of the first recorded instance of the word *cool* and a reference to my mother appearing in the same sentence.

"I think that just about does it," Ivy said.

"What? It's done?" I asked, crouching back down behind her.

"I think so," Miko said. "Here are all the pages in thumbnails. I was working on the Pitch In article in a separate file, so I just need to import that page."

She hit a few buttons, and a new thumbnail appeared, but it was covered by a transparent blue shadow.

"Wait? What?" Miko said. "It looks like this is only a ghost file."

"What's a ghost file?" Tally asked.

"Hang on," Miko said as she typed in a command. The entire magazine disappeared from the screen.

"What happened? Where did it go?" I asked.

"I don't know!" Miko exclaimed. "It's like I accidentally deleted the whole thing, but I'm not sure how."

"Was it saved? Miko, tell me the Pitch In article was saved," Ivy said.

"I don't know," Miko said very quietly. "I don't specifically remember saving it."

"Our work got deleted?" Tally cried, smacking both hands on her head.

"Of course not. It didn't, did it?" I asked, my voice coming out much higher and louder than I realized. I sounded panicked. But we were so close . . . we couldn't fail now.

Miko held her hands up. "Just . . . nobody touch anything. Let me think!"

We all started making suggestions at once, at the same time my door swung open. Kevin stood there accusingly in his pajamas and robe.

"What are you guys flipping out about?" he asked. "Did you find my spider? His name is Phil."

"We might have accidentally deleted a file we've just put two hours of work into," I said, trying to sound calm.

Kevin's eyebrows shot up, and he scurried over and knelt next to me. "Really? Let me see," he said.

"No!" Ivy barked.

Kevin's face fell, and Ivy touched his arm.

"Sorry," she said. "It's really nice of you to want to help, but we've got to make sure we know what we're doing."

"Just undo your last command," Kevin said.

"I know," Ivy said, "but first we need to make sure—"

Before anyone had a chance to react, Kevin reached out and hit two keys.

"KEVIN!" I screeched.

Kevin practically leaped a foot off the ground. "What?" he wailed.

"Yes! It's back!" I heard Miko exclaim.

"It is?" I asked.

"Save it," Ivy said quickly.

"I am," Miko said. "And I'm going to back up a copy to the flash drive right now."

"Told you," Kevin said smugly.

I was so relieved, I threw my arms around my brother and hugged him.

"Ew!" he yelled, wiggling away from me and struggling to his feet. "Cut it out!"

"I think my heart actually stopped for a moment," Tally said, clutching her chest for emphasis.

"I'm going back to bed," Kevin said. "Let me know if you find Phil."

I couldn't let myself start wondering why Kevin had any reason to suspect that the revolting, oversized wolf spider he had adopted might be in my room. I was in the mood to celebrate.

"We did it," Ivy said. "Guys, we actually did it!"

Miko held the flash drive in the air.

"And the whole thing is backed up right here," she said.

"What a relief," Tally said. "That was sooo exhausting."

A heavy wave of fatigue flooded through me all at once. "I'm tired, too," I said.

Ivy yawned. "I think I may actually already be asleep," she said.

She scooted a few feet across the floor and grabbed

her sleeping bag, which she unrolled. Tally did the same, as did Miko, after closing her laptop and stashing it safely on my bookshelf.

I was about to close my laptop, too, when I heard a familiar ringing.

I hesitated for a second, maybe two. But then I reached out and hit the flashing ANSWER VIDEO CALL button. Evelyn appeared on my screen.

"Hey!" she said. "I know it's late, and I only have a second. I just wanted to find out what happened with the Alara the Hun thing. Have you heard back from Finley yet?"

Wow. After the back and forth with Evelyn this weekend, I had completely forgotten to e-mail her that we'd gotten the green light.

"We're fine! She told us there's no problem," I said.

"What a relief!" Evelyn exclaimed, then she grinned. "Were you all freaking out? The PQuits must have been beside themselves! Did—"

"Surprise, look who's here!" I said brightly. Then I spun the computer so the screen and the webcam faced the rest of the room. Ivy and Miko looked curiously at the screen. Tally was facedown in her sleeping bag and appeared to have already fallen into a deep sleep.

"Ev, say hi to Ivy, Tally, and Miko!" I said, emphasizing the last name a little louder than I probably needed to. I leaned around so I could see the screen, too. Evelyn's eyes and mouth had both gone very round. She leaned toward her computer and peered intensely, like the fortune-teller in *The Wizard of Oz* staring into her crystal ball.

"Is that the famous Evelyn? Nice to meet you at last," Ivy called. "Paulina sings your praises every single day."

"Hey, Evelyn," Miko added. "How's the new school?"

Tally snored.

I turned my laptop back toward me. "Work party," I said. "Long, crazy story. Can I call you tomorrow after school?"

Evelyn's surprised look had been replaced by a huge yawn. "Yep," she said. "You better. You are full of surprises, Paulina M. Barbosa."

"Yeah," I agreed. "Good night."

Within seconds, I had stowed my computer, turned out the overhead light, and crawled under the covers.

"Night, everyone," I said.

"Sleep tight," Ivy murmured.

"See you guys in the morning," Miko said. "Then someone can tell me what a PQuit is," she added very quietly.

Oops!

The last thing I was aware of was the low sound of soft breathing and an occasional snorish rumble from Tally's direction.

I would have made a snarky comment about the snoring but felt myself sinking into sleep before I could make the effort. Bizarrely, I had a dream that I was in a softball game, and I'd just stepped up to the plate, hoping like crazy I was about to hit one out of the park.

chapter 16

PITCHING IN FOR PITCH IN

We've got issues at Bixby Middle School, just like kids at any school do. One of the most talked about issues this month is our new softball team and their need for the same kind of funding and attention the other sports teams get.

We may be a small town, but our girls' soccer and basketball teams are some of the best in the county. Last year, ten talented athletes banded together to form Bixby Middle School's first-ever girls' softball team. That same year, a boys' lacrosse team was organized. Those lacrosse players all have new sticks and pads and uniforms this year, but the girls have had to make their own T-shirts and are using their own mitts and old bats and balls. The girls deserve better. That is our opinion.

It is also the law. Did you know that there was legislation passed by Congress in 1972 requiring equal opportunities in school for everyone, including athletic programs? The law is called Title IX, and it still applies today. We've made a lot of progress since 1972, but we still have a ways to go.

Times are tough for schools. We keep hearing there are fewer funds available for our clubs and our field trips and our nonacademic programs. Now more than ever, we have to stay involved and fight to keep the programs we need and love.

Because of the Curriculum Education Project, girls are getting a chance to do something. You all know by now that a group called Pitch In was organized to apply for the CEP money. We've heard their arguments, we've visited their website, and we've learned about everything that their CEP group has to offer. Four of us organized a group, too, to write and publish the magazine you are now reading. In the last few weeks, we've learned a lot about the reality of competition when girls go up against girls. We've also learned a lot about ourselves. And some of what we learned surprised us. In the end, we had to remind one another that the most important thing to remember is everybody deserves to be heard, because we're all in this together.

Check out Pitch In yourself this week. We think it's important you hear what they have to say.

We've come a long way. And one thing is for certain: We are all in this together. And you know what? We're glad to have the company.

We were each supposed to be stationed at a main school entrance on Friday first thing in the morning to hand out copies of *4 Girls,* hot off the presses. While the principal and faculty had the weekend to go over projects, student voting was Friday afternoon. We had to make sure as many kids as possible read the magazine before then. The sight of the cover gave me the same combination of thrill and nervous stomach that it had the evening before when the four of us had seen it for the first time outside the print shop.

"The moment of truth," Ivy had declared, when she had brought the box out of the store to where we had been waiting on the sidewalk.

We had ripped the box open right then and there, each of us grabbing a glossy copy. The magazine had been heavier than I thought it would be but also thinner. I traced my finger over the green lettering on the cover, then had opened to the first page where Miko had created a credits page and listed all of our names.

Paulina M. Barbosa, Editor.

I had felt a surge of pride. Everyone was going to see it! Followed by a surge of terror. *Everyone* was going to see it . . .

"The artwork reproduced beautifully," Ivy had said. "Props to you, Miko. No matter what anyone says, people do judge by the cover, and this one rocks."

"Thanks," Miko replied. "How did you find a printer that stayed in our budget? This is really good quality."

"Wheeling and dealing," Ivy had said.

"We are famous!" Tally cheered. "Every person in school is going to be talking about us tomorrow."

Which brought me in a terrifying bump back to reality.

To stand there at school and physically hand people copies of my . . . creation, my *baby,* for everyone to flip through and smudge and judge . . . I was unprepared for how utterly nerve-racking it was. I tried not to think about it as a bus pulled up in the drop-off circle and a stream of students emerged. I focused on hands, not faces, and gave a copy to every person who walked by me, both girls and boys.

"Hey, check out *4 Girls.* Free copies! Did you get one? Here you go. Remember the vote is this afternoon!"

A tiny sixth-grader stopped for a copy. She looked

at the magazine, then back at me with wide eyes.

"All my friends have been talking about this," she said. "Ever since we heard four girls were making a magazine. Are you one of the four?"

I felt a sudden flame of pride, and I nodded.

"I am," I told her. "I'm one of the four."

The girl smiled and clutched the magazine to her chest. There were more people coming, so I got back to handing out copies.

I didn't go inside until my box was empty. I could see Tally still stationed at the south door, laughing and waving copies in the air as people gathered around her to get their own.

Once I'd finished distributing my copies, I was relieved to get into school. I headed for my locker. On the way, I passed a table set up with a Pitch In banner tacked to the wall behind it. Sasha and Alara were standing by the display. There was a laptop set up showing their video and more flyers and T-shirts.

"Stop and watch our video! Come to our practice this afternoon! Vote Pitch In today!"

Sasha and Alara both looked up as I passed. If I'd had any more copies of 4 *Girls*, I would have tossed a few on their table. But I didn't. Whatever. We'd made plenty of copies and by the end of the day they would be everywhere. Sasha and Alara would see the magazine. I was sure of that.

I grabbed the books I needed for social studies and headed for the stairs. I ran into Miko on the landing.

"How weird was that, handing out copies?" Miko asked me.

"Very weird," I agreed. "It was, like, basically saying to the entire school, 'Judge me!'"

"Yeah," she said. "Which is exactly what they're going to do when they vote. Waiting until Monday for the results is killer. This is going to be the longest weekend of my life."

I hadn't even thought of that.

"You're right. It's going to feel like it's dragging out forever," I said.

The second bell rang, and Miko started moving past me.

"Yeah, text me if it starts getting to you," she said. "Later."

"You too," I replied after a startled moment. Probably too late for her to hear—she was already gone.

I jogged up the stairs and was halfway through the classroom door when another bell rang in high, short bursts.

You had to be kidding me. The fire alarm?

I could immediately see by Ms. Zangeist's unworried expression and the fact that she was still wearing her coat and scarf that the alarm was a preplanned drill.

She stood balancing on her crutches, holding up her recently broken foot. I turned around and filed back into the hall and down the stairs with everyone else. Tally loomed up next to me like a whirlwind, looking excited. She was wearing a turquoise ball cap and a pair of purple hoop earrings so large you could have fit a tennis ball through them.

"What do you think is on fire?" she asked. "I hope our magazines don't get burned up. Should I wear this hat or not? There are going to be firemen everywhere!"

"I don't think anything is on fire," I said. "It's a drill."

Tally's face fell.

"Oh," she said.

During fire drills, each grade had a designated waiting area in the playground. Once we checked in with whatever teacher was holding the clipboard, we were free to mingle and chat as long as we stayed with our grade. I used to enjoy the little break from routine, but today all I could see were people leafing through copies of *4 Girls*. My work. Being examined and discussed.

I was trying to pretend I didn't notice Shelby Simpson and Daphne Minsk reading a shared copy, their heads bent together. Seventh-graders were still arriving to check in. I looked down at my shoes.

Benny would be out here somewhere. I didn't want to see him—not during another fire drill. Ever since the slumber party when Miko said that he liked me, I'd felt incredibly awkward when I saw him. Because if Miko Suzuki said somebody liked you, it had to be true.

"Excellent timing," Ivy said, appearing without warning at my elbow.

"Why?" I asked, zipping up my coat. It was chilly in the shade. I liked cool, crisp fall days, and as I took a deep breath, I knew the seasons had changed. Summer was over. And fall was off to a great start.

"Gives everyone that much more time to read and discuss," Ivy said.

"I guess, but I don't want to stand here watching it," I told her.

I had been observing Tally circulate through the crowd. Now she veered off and joined us. "Well, you were right," she said sadly. "No fire. No firemen."

"Think positive," Ivy said. "Tomorrow is another day. Another chance for something to burn down."

"I hope so." Tally sighed. "And in the meantime, we are totally famous, y'all. I heard so many people talking about us!"

"Saying what?" Ivy asked.

"No, don't say," I interrupted. "I don't want to know."

A final group of seventh-graders arrived, Miko among them. I waved to her in a little "come on over here" gesture. She waved back, but she'd also seen Shelby and Daphne. She made a face that more or less expressed "sorry" and went to stand with her friends.

Oh well.

Ivy was watching me. "Rome wasn't built in a day," she remarked.

Tally had produced a banana from her coat pocket and was peeling it.

"People always say that, and I never know what it means," she said, taking a bite of banana. "I mean, how long did it take to build Rome then?"

"It just means that big things don't happen all at once," I said, casting another sidelong glance at the PQuits. Charelle had joined them. Shelby was holding up the cover of *4 Girls* and talking excitedly. At least they didn't seem to be trashing it.

Tally looked back and forth between me and Ivy. "But how long *did* it take?" she repeated.

Ivy just laughed, the sound suddenly eclipsed by the blare of the all-clear siren. Kids who'd come outside without their coats bolted toward the building.

"One period mostly down, eight to go," Ivy said.

"I'm never going to make it through this day," I said.

• • • • • • •

But somehow I did. I kept my head down. I wimped out at lunch, choosing to go to the library rather than the ultra-public cafeteria. I was way too nervous to be hungry, anyway. My stomach was growling louder than it ever had before, but there was no way I was going to eat anything.

Finally, after eighth period, the announcement came over the PA system that ballots were now available by the office and that students should be taking the next period to make their final decisions on the CEP groups and cast their votes.

I headed over to the office as soon as I heard the announcement, figuring maybe I could get my vote cast without anyone seeing me. But there were already fifteen or so people milling about when I got there. So much for my stealth mode.

"Good luck, Paulina," called an eighth-grader whose name suddenly disappeared from my brain.

"Thanks," I said, ducking my head and swinging by the table. I grabbed one of the ballots without slowing down, then retreated to a quieter spot by the water fountain, where I looked at it for the first time.

Curriculum Education Project Student Voting Form

Only one vote per student will be accepted.

Vote for only one project. Ballots that do not contain both the voter's first *and* last names, or that vote for multiple projects, will be disqualified.

Results of this vote will not solely determine the winner of the Curriculum Education Project but will be taken into serious consideration by the faculty and administration in the decision process.

Name:
Grade:

<CHECK ONE BOX ONLY>
[ ] CHICK LIT book group
[ ] GIRLS CARE child-sponsor program
[ ] *4 GIRLS* magazine
[ ] PITCH IN softball team

I filled out the form, checked the *4 Girls* box, and folded the paper in half. The crowd had temporarily thinned near the table holding the ballot box, so I swooped by and dunked my ballot in. It got stuck, half in, half out, and hung there mortifying me. I doubled back and shoved it down the slot.

Now I just wanted to escape—to have it be time to get on the bus and away from school. To play my iPod. To indulge myself. *Ring Dings,* I thought. *That's what I want. And cappuccinos.*

At that moment, I saw Sasha Hendricks and Alara Jameson coming down the hall toward the office. Sasha had a copy of *4 Girls* tucked under her arm. She pointed at me with her free hand. "Hey. I want to talk to you," she said.

Okay. It had been a very long day, and I was headed into an even longer weekend. I just wasn't in the mood for this. But Sasha had stopped right in front of me, and I wasn't getting by her unless I went for a football-style body tackle. I decided staying to listen would cause less damage in the end.

"The . . . we . . . ," Sasha began. "You . . ."

But she found her words after the three false starts. "This thing you did. This article."

She held up her copy of *4 Girls,* like it might need clarifying—like it might be any one of a vast number of articles about her team written by me.

I nodded.

"It was a cool thing for you to do," Sasha said.

"Thanks," I replied, with a quick peek at Alara. Alara looked irritated. I resisted the overwhelming urge to stick my tongue out at her. "It was everybody's idea—all four of us."

Sasha gave a small nod. "Look, Polly, I was wrong about you. I believed you guys were cheaters. I forwarded that blog link to everybody on my team—volleyball, too, because I was sure you weren't playing fair."

She was also wrong about my name, but far be it from me to point it out.

"To be honest, I still wasn't convinced after you posted Finley's response. But this"—she waved the magazine at me—"this shows me you four are stand-up girls."

"I'm glad you think so," I said. "I didn't feel like we had to be enemies because of one anonymous blog post."

I cast a glance at Alara when I said *anonymous*. Sasha gave Alara a quick scowl, enough to convince me that Sasha knew, or at least suspected, the source of the post, too.

"Well, when I make a mistake, I own it," Sasha stated. "I've already e-mailed everyone I know to say so."

"That's great. We all appreciate it," I said. "Good

luck on Monday, Sasha."

She gave me another quick nod.

"Thanks," she said, resuming her walk toward the office.

"You too, Alara," I called. "Good luck."

Alara must have heard me, but she didn't turn around or acknowledge what I'd said.

Oh well, I thought. *Rome wasn't built in a day.*

· chapter ·
17

The special assembly was scheduled during first period on Monday. I wasn't big on Monday mornings, but at least there'd be no drawn-out waiting.

The four of us made a plan to get to school a half hour early and meet in room 107 to have a little private time before the big announcement. Ivy was already there when I arrived. Given the early hour, Ivy looked amazingly unrumpled in a green turtleneck and a kilt fastened with a skull pin.

"I brought doughnuts," Ivy said, looking at her feet.

No good morning, or how are you. *She's nervous,* I thought. *But who isn't?*

"Flaxseed muffins," I said, holding the bag in the air. "My mother bought them herself."

Miko and Tally came in a minute later. Miko had a jug of cider and another of milk.

"Oh no!" Tally exclaimed when she saw the food.

"I had bagels, and I left them in the car!"

"Don't worry," I assured her. "We have a ton of food here, and I am even less hungry than I was on Friday."

"I know, right?" Miko agreed. "We should just leave all this stuff in the faculty break room."

"Oh, they'd love us," Ivy said. "But Alara would probably accuse us of offering them a bribe."

"Ha, you're right. So less than a half hour to go," I said. "I still want to win as badly as ever, but I also am so ready for this limbo to be over."

Tally let out a sudden, short scream. "I left my book bag in the car, too!" she wailed.

"Call your mother and ask her to come back," Miko suggested.

"Oh, she will," Tally said. "I don't need to call her. She always notices as soon as she gets to our driveway, and she brings it into the office."

"How often do you leave your book bag in the car, Tal?" Ivy asked.

"Oh, not that often," she said. "It's only because I'm so crazy nervous about the announcement. This is only the second time I forgot this year."

For the first month of school, maybe that was an improvement for Tally.

"Well, one way or the other, we'll know by the end of the morning," Ivy reassured her.

Tally shook her head.

"It isn't just *4 Girls*. Audriana found out our fall showcase is going to be *Annie*! I have only wanted to play that part my entire life. Auditions are next week. It's going to be like World War Broadway until tryouts. We have to do a story about it in the next *4 Girls*."

"If there is a next *4 Girls*," Miko said. "The buzz is a lot of people voted for Pitch In."

"A lot of people voted for us, too," Ivy said. "I'm not giving up. You know what would be great for the next issue? A comic strip. Doesn't that girl with the superlong hair do comics?"

"And book reviews," I added. "They'd be awesome."

"I'm a sucker for a good personality quiz," Miko chimed in.

Once we all got talking, the butterflies retreated from my stomach enough for me to take a bite of a glazed doughnut. I was thinking how good it tasted when the bell rang and I dropped the doughnut right on the table.

"I guess it's time," Ivy said. "We can swing by and clear this stuff later."

We all stood up, but for a moment, no one moved. We just looked at one another.

"Hey, guys? Whatever happens, we did something amazing together," I said. "On Friday this girl asked if I was one of the four. It felt really good to say yes."

"The Four," Ivy said.

"The Four," Miko repeated. She bit her lower lip.

An extremely impatient squeal escaped from Tally's mouth.

"Can 'the four' please get moving?" she asked.

Yes. No. Maybe.

"I'm ready," I said. I walked to the door and opened it. The others each filed through, and I took one final peek at the room and its breakfast-filled table before pulling the door shut so Ivy could lock it.

● ● ● ● ● ● ●

The auditorium seemed even noisier than usual.

People are just psyched to be missing first period, I thought. *It's not like everyone else has been on pins and needles all weekend. Just us and Sasha's crew.*

The four of us sat together in the second-to-last row. By this time, all of us, even Tally, seemed too overwhelmed with anticipation or nerves to talk.

I hate competitions, I thought.

But at least I wasn't alone. Three people sitting next to me knew almost exactly how I felt. I don't know why, but the fact that I wasn't in it alone made it better.

The chattering died away when Mrs. Finley appeared and walked up to the podium. The only sound remaining was coughing, the occasional whisper, and the squeaking sound of people fidgeting in their seats.

"Good morning," Mrs. Finley said into the microphone. "I have a few quick announcements. Math tutoring will be held next Thursday instead of Monday, for that week only, in room 213. The C bus is undergoing maintenance, so students who take that bus please look for a different one. There will be a sign posted, and you will have your regular bus driver. Please do not go to the office and tell them your bus is not there."

I began wiggling my foot nervously. I didn't wish confusion on the innocent students of the C bus, but come on. Couldn't we get on with it already?

"Okay, so let's get to the real reason for this assembly," Mrs. Finley said as if I'd spoken out loud. "To reveal the results of the Curriculum Education Project."

An outbreak of applause erupted from the audience. Mrs. Finley ignored it.

"We had a wide variety of projects submitted over the summer, and we narrowed them down to four finalists," she said. "By now you are familiar with all of them: a book club, a softball team, a magazine, and a child-sponsorship program. All of them are organizations proposed and produced by girls, with the intent of enhancing the lives of other girls. I've been extremely pleased with the results of this competition."

More clapping. I wiggled my foot harder.

"The student vote was counted on Friday, and the faculty and administration had a special meeting Sunday afternoon. The results point overwhelmingly to two projects. By count of the student vote, Pitch In and *4 Girls* are more or less in tying position."

My wiggling foot suddenly froze. Ivy and I exchanged a look.

"So it fell to us to determine a winner. An extremely difficult choice to say the least. I think the results will surprise you.

"So without further delay, I'm pleased to announce the winner of the Curriculum Education Project, our newest fully funded student organization."

I held my breath. Ivy reached out and grabbed my hand, and I squeezed as hard as I could.

"The winner is *4 Girls*!"

The room broke into applause, and a whoop of surprised happiness escaped my mouth. I looked down the aisle at my friends. Tally was literally bouncing up and down in her chair until she turned to deliver a crushing hug to Miko, who was staring straight ahead with her mouth wide open. Ivy was sitting up very straight, her face shining. She looked at me and winked, and I started to laugh. None of it seemed real.

As if from a huge distance, I heard Mrs. Finley's voice.

"Quiet please," she ordered. "I did say that I thought the results would surprise you, and I haven't explained that yet."

The residual clapping and murmuring died away. She had everyone's full attention.

"Thank you," the principal said. "I was not the only person moved by the decision *4 Girls* made to feature Pitch In on their cover. Every principal wishes for that level of camaraderie in their students, but we don't often have the pleasure of seeing it. On Saturday, I received a phone call at home from Larry Novak, the owner of our local Planet Sports store. His grandson had just showed him the magazine."

Whoa. She had to be talking about Benny. What was going on?

"Mr. Novak read the issue of *4 Girls*, and then he made a remarkable offer. Because of his generosity, and what the school is additionally willing to provide, Pitch In will also receive funding for uniforms, bats, gloves, and rotating use of the main playing field and school bus. So I'm delighted to tell you that we have two real winners!"

The kids went wild, clapping and hooting and stamping their feet.

Ivy poked me in the arm.

"It's official. The guy *likes* you," she declared.

"Will the creators of *4 Girls* please stand up?"

Mrs. Finley asked.

Tally had already shot to her feet. Ivy and I stood up, too, followed by Miko, who still looked fairly stunned.

"And the members of Pitch In, please stand also," Mrs. Finley added.

Around the room, Sasha and ten or twelve other girls stood up, too, several of them hooting and high-fiving one another. From where I was standing, I suddenly caught sight of Benny, who had turned around in his seat and was looking at me.

I couldn't do anything but smile. I smiled at everybody. I smiled at Miko and the PQuits. And though it took over a year, I finally smiled at Benny Novak.

Ivy threw an arm around me, and I grabbed her in a jubilant hug.

"And now the fun really begins," she said, loudly enough to be heard over the din.

I was so wrung out from the stress and the work and the waiting. I was more than ready for fun. I wished that I could Skype Evelyn right now because I couldn't wait to see the look on her face when she heard what Benny Novak had done. And when I told her I'd finally managed to smile at the guy.

But for the moment, surrounded by clapping and cheering, I was also perfectly happy to be right here. At school.

A feeling like that doesn't come around too often.

· chapter ·
18

I felt like my stomach might burst.

I pushed the sundae dish away, then pulled it back to retrieve a few more chunks of peanut butter cup, which I popped in my mouth. Then I pushed the dish away again.

"And when she said the thing about the surprise, I was, like, how can there be a surprise? Isn't finding out the winner a surprise?" Tally was talking rapidly, waving her spoon around in the air. "And so I— Paulina, are you going to finish that?"

I groaned.

"My stomach was finished ten minutes ago. Unfortunately, my taste buds didn't get the message. Has anyone ever been hospitalized from eating too much peanut butter cup banana cream pie sundae?" I asked.

"With extra nuts," Ivy pointed out helpfully.

I groaned again.

"You didn't even eat the whole thing," Miko pointed out, pulling a napkin from the dispenser and rubbing at a splotch of ice cream that had dripped onto the table in front of her.

"Well, you barely ate half of yours," I said, pointing at Miko's dish.

"Mine was bigger," Miko said.

"I still just can't believe today happened!" Tally said, shaking her head.

"It did happen," Miko said, draping her napkin gently over the rest of her sundae like she was putting it to bed.

"We earned it," Ivy said, scooping at the bottom of her bowl for the last remnants of cookie dough ice cream.

"So did Pitch In," I added. "Who would have imagined it would work out for both of us?"

"What I wonder," Tally said, "is if the faculty would have picked us to win if the Planet Sports guy hadn't made his offer."

The question provoked an instant silence at the table.

"That would mean we'd owe the win to Benny Novak," Ivy said, giving me a look. "He did it for love."

"Maybe we won the tiebreaker because we did the cover story on Pitch In," I said, directing the subject away from Benny Novak. "Mrs. Finley did say how moved she was that we did that. Might have tipped the scales in our favor."

Miko's phone rang, her ringtone a new song I recognized but couldn't name. Miko flipped the phone open.

"Hi. Yep. Yeah, I know. I'm not, Shel. It's just a quick meeting, but my mother will have a fit if I don't go straight home. I'll text you later, 'kay?"

She snapped the phone shut.

"Sorry," she said.

"Or maybe they picked us because we're four talented people who put together an amazing magazine in a really short amount of time, in spite of the fact that we barely knew each other three weeks ago. Maybe they realized we've created something that's really important to girls," Ivy stated.

"Well, we'll never know for sure, and it doesn't even matter. The point is, we won," I said. I picked up my spoon, then put it down again. "We did a ton of work to get the issue together, and now we have to start all over again and get started on the next one. I'm thinking we should try to do it as a monthly, so we'd have to plan for the end of October. Are we all ready?"

"I'm actually not sure I can do it," Miko said.

There was a silence around the table.

"You mean you're quitting?" Ivy asked.

"No. Maybe. Look, I'm just not sure, okay?" Miko said. "I have a lot going on, and getting the magazine done took up a ton of time."

"Yes, but we won!" I said. "So your parents should be happy, right? They should want you to keep working on it."

"It's complicated," Miko said. "I have a lot of stuff going on."

"No, I know," I said. "But you found the time for the first issue, and now that we sort of know what we're doing, you—"

"I said it was complicated, okay?" Miko snapped. "Are you suddenly the expert on how I should budget my time?"

"She didn't say that," Ivy said. "But would it help if we said something to your parents, like, as a group, to—"

"No! Just drop it!" Miko exclaimed. "I said I have a lot going on. I did the design work you needed, the issue is out, and the rest of my life is none of your business."

There was an uncomfortable silence. What was anyone supposed to say to that?

Miko's phone chirped again. She opened it, glanced at the screen, then snapped it shut like she wanted to break it.

"I have to go," she said, getting up.

"Bye," I said quietly.

Miko hesitated for a fraction of a second then shoved her phone in her purse and bolted out of the door. I watched through the window as she climbed into a car waiting outside.

"Nice," Ivy said.

"Wait, y'all, did Miko just quit?" Tally asked. "Or am I missing something as usual?"

"She just quit," Ivy confirmed.

"We don't know that," I argued. "She said she wasn't sure."

Ivy gave me a look. "She quit," Ivy repeated.

"But then what are we going to do?" Tally said.

"We'll figure it out," I said.

"Yeah, we know what we're doing now," Ivy added. "If we could get the first issue out in three weeks, we can do anything."

Tally didn't look convinced.

Frankly, I wasn't, either. Yes, we had experience now, but that didn't mean we had Miko's knack for art and design. Some things couldn't be faked.

"Yep, we'll figure it out," I repeated.

Tally's phone went off in an electronic, sped-up rendition of "Somewhere Over the Rainbow."

"Maybe my ride is here now," Tally said, picking up her phone. "Except I told my mother I was walking home." She read a message, and her normally sunny expression darkened.

"You have got to be kidding me," Tally said through clenched teeth.

"Not your mother?" Ivy guessed.

"What's wrong?" I asked.

"This is terrible, y'all. I just got some really bad news."

"What is it?" I tried to sound casual, but I was worried. Tally looked as though she was about to burst into tears. She took a deep breath. "Buster just texted me that Valerie Teale is telling everyone she's auditioning for the part of Annie, too, and that she has a new voice coach who was in the original Broadway cast and knows the insider secrets and tricks to the part because she went on four times as understudy." Tally shook her head as she spoke, like maybe if she did that hard enough she could make the news go away.

"Is that all?" Ivy asked. "I thought someone had been in a car accident or something."

"*Is that all?*" Tally repeated. "Do you have any idea what this means? If Valerie Teale is telling the truth, this drama coach is, like, her ace in the mole!"

Ivy looked at me. I gave her an I-have-no-idea shrug.

"Ace in the hole," Ivy said quietly.

"Exactly!" Tally exclaimed. "I mean, is that even legal?"

"Having a voice coach?" I asked. "I think it's legal."

"Well, it shouldn't be," Tally declared. "I am so tired of Valerie Teale stealing my parts with her special coaches and her shrieky voice and her awful bug eyes. Y'all, I've gotta get home and call Audriana," Tally said, standing up so quickly that the entire booth seemed to wobble. "I'm sorry, but this is war."

"It's okay," Ivy said. "We all probably need to get going."

"Hey, don't make yourself crazy over this, Tally," I said. "Remember—you won the CEP competition today! You're on a roll. You're going to get that part."

Tally shook her head as she pulled two mismatched gloves out of her bag.

"I hope you're right," she said. "Because if I don't get that part, my entire life will be ruined, and I will never feel happiness again, and I will waste away alone and defeated and die of misery and despair. Anyway, see y'all tomorrow!"

She brushed her hair out of her face and bounced bravely toward the door. Ivy and I exchanged a look.

"Let's hope The Four aren't about to turn into The Two," she said.

I nodded, sighing. "We'll figure it out," I said for the third time. Even I did not sound like I believed me.

"Paulie, of course we'll figure it out," Ivy said. "Don't look so worried."

A phone beeped. Mine this time. I flipped it open.

"It's Kevin," I told Ivy. "I'm supposed to walk home with him at eight. Apparently, I'm four minutes late. Fortunately, he's still sitting right behind us."

Ivy grinned then swiveled around to face the booth directly behind her. "Sorry. She'll be right with you."

Kevin popped into view like a gopher coming out of a hole. "I hope so, because I'm going to miss the special they're showing on *Battlestar Galactica* unless we leave now," he said.

"I love *Battlestar Galactica*," Ivy said.

"You do?" asked Kevin. He disappeared for a minute, scrambled out of his booth, and stood next to our table. "Seriously?"

"Now you can be seen talking to us in public?" I asked. "Because Ivy likes *Battlestar Galactica*?"

"Yep," Kevin said.

"Yes, I seriously like *Battlestar*," Ivy said. "I'm more into *Stargate* and *Dr. Who*, though."

At the mention of two of his all-time favorite sci-fi programs, Kevin's mouth dropped open and he stared at Ivy like she was a rock star.

"But you're . . . a girl," he said.

"He is a bright one," Ivy said to me as she stood up. "How proud you must be."

"I pinch myself every day to make sure I'm not dreaming," I assured her.

"I was going to watch that *BG* special, too," Ivy said. "You guys ready to go?"

"Yep," I said. "Let's go, Kev."

We walked outside together, Kevin still staring at Ivy with a kind of awe.

"Are you getting a ride?" I asked Ivy.

She nodded, pulling out a phone. "My mother told me to call when I was ready," she said.

"Do you want us to wait with you?"

Ivy smiled. "Thanks, but I'm fine. We don't want Kevin to miss any of the show."

"Okay. I guess I'll see you tomorrow then."

Ivy gave me a hug.

"We did it, Paulina M. Barbosa," Ivy said.

"We did," I said. "But—"

"And we'll do it again," she interrupted. "Do not worry, okay?"

"I'm not worried," I said loudly. "We'll figure it out."

"Yep," Ivy said. "Now try to look like you believe it. Listen, my mom says you're welcome to come for a sleepover on Friday. Just the two of us."

"That would be great," I said. "I'll ask my mom, but I'm sure it will be fine."

"Cool. See you tomorrow!" Ivy waved and flipped open her cell phone.

"Come on," I told my brother. "If we walk fast we can be home in ten minutes."

"Hurry then," Kevin said.

"You hurry," I said as we started walking.

"So since you and that girl are friends now, will she be coming over more?" Kevin asked.

"You mean Ivy?" I said.

He nodded, looking at his shoes.

Was his face turning red? I pretended to be fascinated by a couple of birds flying overhead.

"I'm sure she will," I said.

"Oh. Well, that'll probably be okay," Kevin said.

"Good to know I have your permission," I said. "And 4 Girls appreciates it. Hey, you never told me what you thought of it. You read a copy, right?"

"Ew, no," Kevin said. "It's girl stuff."

"Doesn't mean you can't read it," I said. "It's not all about dresses and lip gloss, you know."

"Yeah, but what's in there that boys would want to read?" Kevin asked. "Maybe you should do reviews of sci-fi stuff. I would read it then."

"That's not a bad idea," I told him. "You know what, Kev, I kind of like it. Maybe after your show you could write down a couple of ideas."

"Okay," Kevin said. "As soon as I finish my homework. And find Phil."

He picked up the pace suddenly.

"As soon as you what? Who's Phil?"

"My spider," Kevin called over his shoulder.

"Kevin!" I yelled. "Do you mean to tell me that you never found that spider?"

Kevin was practically jogging now—a good fifteen feet ahead of me.

I gave up trying to catch up to my little brother, then suddenly I started to laugh out loud. I laughed and laughed.

It wasn't so much that I hated spiders—it was surprises that I hated. And spiders in houses, especially ones the size of Phil, had a way of surprising people.

But life was full of surprises, some of them fabulous and some of them hairy with eight legs. It's just the way it was, and I was surprised at how okay I was with that.

I picked up the pace, though Kevin was still way ahead of me. I couldn't wait to video chat with Evelyn tonight and see her face as I ran through the events of the day: how we had won the competition and Miko had possibly quit and Tally was potentially going to theater war before perishing of despair and that Phil was missing and that, on top of all that, I had finally smiled at Benny Novak.

The day Evelyn moved away I'd been so convinced that I'd never have fun at school again.

And yet, I'd just had one of the best days I could remember in a long time.

The Four might be down a girl with a second

possibly about to become a basket case. *Annie* was coming up and Halloween and Homecoming. Before I knew it, the next issue of *4 Girls* would be due, along with midterms and dances. How would it all get done?

I'll figure it out, I thought.

And finally I believed that I would. Though there would probably be plenty more drama—and suspense—and some unexpected twists and turns.

If I'd learned one thing this month, it was that great things could happen even when things did not go the way you planned. *Especially* when they didn't.

I was ready for any and all surprises and keeping my options open along the way.

ABOUT THE AUTHOR

Elizabeth Cody Kimmel is a widely published author of thirty books for children and young adults, including *The Reinvention of Moxie Roosevelt* and the *Suddenly Supernatural* and *Lily B.* series. Elizabeth is proud to admit that she was never asked to sit at the Prom-Queens-in-Training table in her middle-school cafeteria. She likes reading, hiking, peanut butter cups, and *Star Trek*, but not at the same time. You can visit her at www.codykimmel.com.